William Winter, George Arnold

The poems of George Arnold

William Winter, George Arnold

The poems of George Arnold

ISBN/EAN: 9783744770521

Printed in Europe, USA, Canada, Australia, Japan

Cover: Foto ©Andreas Hilbeck / pixelio.de

More available books at **www.hansebooks.com**

THE POEMS

OF

GEORGE ARNOLD.

COMPLETE EDITION.

EDITED, WITH A BIOGRAPHICAL SKETCH OF THE POET,

By WILLIAM WINTER.

BOSTON:

JAMES R. OSGOOD AND COMPANY.

1880.

CONTENTS.

	PAGE
SKETCH OF GEORGE ARNOLD (1866)	9
PREFACE TO POEMS GRAVE AND GAY (1867)	25

DRIFT, AND OTHER POEMS (1866).

DRIFT	41
THE JOLLY OLD PEDAGOGUE	52
RECRIMINATION	57
INTROSPECTION	65
WOOL-GATHERING	73
THE TWO AUTUMNS	79
ALONE BY THE HEARTH	83
THE GARDEN OF MEMORY	86
AN IDYL OF OCTOBER	91
ALL FOR LOVE	96
THE BALLAD OF ROSALIE	99
TRAILING ARBUTUS	102
THE OLD PLACE	105
THE GIFT OF LOVE	106
MIGNON	109
MINNIE'S ANSWER	111

iv   *Contents.*

AU COMBLE 113
SWEET IMPATIENCE 115
AN AUTUMN JOY 119
IN VAIN 122
GONE 124
DE PROFUNDIS 125
A FAREWELL 126
VALE! 128
EXPRESSION 131
THE TRYST 133
AMONG THE HEATHER 135
THE LEES OF LIFE 136
FARCEUR DE POETE! 137
BEER 139
YOUTH AND AGE 142
THE BUTTERFLY AND THE POET 143
CUI BONO? 144
THE GOLDEN FISH 146
ÇA M'EST EGAL! 147
GOLD AND PURPLE 149
PARTING 150
THEN AND NOW 151
LOVE'S MESSENGERS 153
LAZINESS 157
THE SIMPLE RHYME 158
MEADOW-SWEET 160
FAREWELL TO SUMMER 161

Contents. V

September	164
The Heart's Rest	167
The Siren of the Rose	169
On the Sands	171
Foul Weather	173
Apart	174
At Dusk	176
Serenade	178
Via Crucis	180
Christmas Eve	181
New-Year's Eve	184
Jubilate	186
The Matron Year	187
Requiescam	190
In the Dark	192

POEMS GRAVE AND GAY (1867).

I. GRAVE.

A Summer Longing	199
Fire-Flies	201
A Sunset Fantasie	203
Art and Nature	206
Psyche	214
My Wind-Harp	215
Sea-shore Fancies	216

THE OMEN	218
SEPTEMBER DAYS	220
GOLDEN-ROD	222
OCTOBER	224
SUMMER AND AUTUMN	227
THE MERRY CHRISTMAS TIME	229
THE POET'S AWAKENING	232
JACOB'S LADDER	233
HER EYES	235
ENOUGH	236
MIDNIGHT MUSIC	237
WINE SONG	239
SERENADE	241
THE OLD RAMBLE	243
ALONE BY THE SHORE	246
I WANT NOT LOVE	248
IN THE ORGAN-LOFT	249
THE BROKEN CAVALIER'S SONG	251
AN AUTOBIOGRAPHY	253
AT THE CIRCUS	254
DRINKING WINE	257
SONG OF THE SENSUOUS	259
QUAND MÊME	261
AT NEWPORT	269
GLORIA	274
CAMP COGITATIONS	276
JUNE 24, 1859	282
JUNE 24, 1864	284

Contents. vii

II. GAY.

Don Leon's Bride 287
The Big Oyster 297
The Drinking of the Apple-Jack 303
Single and Double 308
The Ballad of Fistiana 315
The Modern Mithridates 320
Patti 323
Piccolomini 325
The Dangers of Broadway 327
The Fourth of July in Town 330
The Sharpshooter's Love 333
The Song of the Stone-Hulk 335
Two Sensible Serenades 337
No More 340
The Common Councilman 343
The Conservative's Lament 346
Queer Weather 350
Facilis Decensus Avenue 352
The Song of the Home Guard 356
A Voice from on Deck 359
The Plaint of the Postage-Stamp 361
The War-Poet's Lament 363
Shoddy 366

GEORGE ARNOLD.

———◆———

THE author of the poems contained in this volume was very dear to me as a comrade, and so I do not pretend to speak impartially of his character and his writings. During a period of six years it was my fortune to be associated with him under a variety of circumstances, and to participate in many of his pleasures and in some of his sorrows. Not many weeks have passed, since all that was mortal of him was laid in the tomb. It may chance, therefore, that tenderness for his memory and grief for his loss will somewhat color the language of this memoir. Affection is not critical. But, whatever be the faults of this attempt to depict the departed poet, I confidently believe that every appreciative reader of these poems will recognize them as the exponents of genius and of a remarkable and winning character.

George Arnold was born in Bedford Street, New York, on the 24th of June, 1834, and died at Strawberry Farms, Monmouth County, New Jersey, on the 9th of November, 1865. The events of his short life were neither numerous nor striking. His parents continued to reside in New York till he was three years of age, when they removed to Alton, in the State of Illinois. There he passed twelve years of his boyhood, — happy, buoyant years, diversified by exercise and study, and blessed by free communication with nature, amidst some of her most picturesque and inspiring scenery. There, doubtless, he laid the foundations of that profound love and genuine knowledge of nature which he manifested in after years. He never went to school. His education was conducted by his parents, from whom he learned, in a happy home, those lessons of truth and fact, and those simple principles of action, which are the sufficient basis of an honorable life. Those teachings he never forgot; and, though his later years were not unblemished with errors, he was, from first to last, in all things and to all persons, straightforward, sincere, and manly. Nor was this result altogether due to early training. Simplicity and truthfulness of character were born attributes of the man. His nature was frank, gentle, and sweet, and all his impulses were generous and good.

In the summer of 1849 his parents removed from Illinois, and settled at Strawberry Farms, in the State of New Jersey. A Fourierite Phalansterie had been established there; but, at this time, it was gradually breaking up. Residing there during the next three years, seeing many social reformers, — some of them peculiarly rational, and some of them peculiarly eccentric, — and hearing continually of social reform, the impressible mind of the young poet took a philosophical bent, and began very early to speculate upon the difference between things as they are

and things as they ought to be. This habit of
thought continued with him to the end of his
life. He was never a reformer, indeed, and for
professional reformers he entertained a cordial
contempt. His conviction appeared to be, — and
it is, perhaps, as sound as any doctrine of con-
temporary social philosophy, — that "the world
is out of joint," and that no mere human power
is available to set it right. With his philosophy,
however, — or his lack of it, — the reader is not
concerned ; and I refer to his youthful acquaintance with reformers and doctrines of reform, only
to explain that bias toward speculation which
appears in certain of his poems, — notably in
"Wool-Gathering," — and that independent men-
tal custom of viewing all subjects through the
eyes of common sense, to which may be attrib-
uted the vigor and freshness of much that he
has written.

In the autumn of 1852, having developed a
strong preference and natural aptitude for the
art of painting, he was placed in the studio of

a portrait-painter in New York. This was the
beginning of his career as a worker in the
fine arts. Experience proved, however, that he
had mistaken his avocation. He speedily became a good draughtsman, and manifested skill
and taste in the department of landscape-paint-
ing. This cleverness in sketching landscapes
grew with his years, and afforded him great enjoyment. Several of his friends possess little
sketches that he made, chiefly in water-colors,
which, if much less complete as works of art,
are often as characteristic of the author as
even his poems themselves. Such a sketch is
before me, as I write these words. It represents
a square in an old German city. Around the
square are quaint houses, with diamond-paned
windows and staring gargoyles. In the back-
ground a cathedral lifts its spire toward the
blue sky of summer, flecked with clouds of
fleece. The lame beggar halts along in the
shadow. Hooded monks stand apart, conversing.
The whole scene is gentle, slumberous, poetic,

and suggestive. But it was oftener with the sweet or stern aspects of nature that the poet's fancy held genial communion. He loved to think of quiet woodland places; of moss-grown rocks, and the bright green of creeping vines; of the musical purl and tinkle of lonely brooks; of thick-clustering, dewy roses; of the burnished glories of autumnal woods; of the wind among the pine-trees, on sombre autumn nights; of lonely beaches, whereon forever echoes the ancient, solemn dirge of the sorrowing, desolate ocean, mindful not alone of its own mysterious grief, but of missing ships, and vanished forms, and "wrecks far out at sea." His poems beautifully manifest these moods of his fancy; and these moods also tinged his little sketches, and gave them a characteristic quality. But he did not succeed as a painter of faces and figures, and so he very soon abandoned the effort to become an artist with the brush. His early studies of painting, however, were not wasted. Loving the art, and knowing its technicalities, he subsequently became an excellent art-critic. His criticisms of paintings, scattered far and wide in the daily and weekly press of New York city, are numerous, and are animated by genuine sympathy with noble and· beautiful ideals, cordial appreciation as well of minor merits as of lofty conceptions, and a frank and hearty contempt for mere prettiness and charlatanism. He was unusually competent for the proper performance of this work, and, as far as is possible in ephemeral journalism, he faithfully served the art in which he had once hoped to win distinction.

The transition from the brush to the pen is not uncommon. With him it was natural and inevitable. Though his temperament was dreamy, his will never became the slave of dreams. He laid down the brush with a sigh ; but he laid it down : and, thenceforward, to the end of his life, he worked with the pen, incurring the perils, bearing the sorrows, surmounting the obstacles, and enjoying the pleasures of the noble and fascinating profession of letters. His literary careei

extended over a period of about. twelve years.
In the course of that time he wrote, with equal
fluency and versatility, stories, sketches, essays,
poems, comic and satirical verses, criticisms of
books and of pictures, editorial articles, jokes
and pointed paragraphs,—everything, in short,
for which there is a demand in the literary magazines of the country, and in New York journalism. The quantity of written material which he
thus produced is surprisingly large. Much of it,
of course, is of an ephemeral character. As is
usual with men of letters, who live by the pen,
Arnold was obliged to combine the profession
of journalism with that of literature ; and in
journalism, sufficient unto the day is the article
thereof. But, while he wrote much for the moment, he wrote much also that will endure. He
was not simply a journalist. The original mind,
the large, warm heart, and the sleepless fire of
genius often gave accidental worth to even his
lightest compositions. In this way "he builded
better than he knew." The reader of his "Mc-

Arone" papers, commenced in "Vanity Fair," November 24, 1860, and continued, in that and other journals, with but slight intermissions, until October 14, 1865, will especially appreciate the truth of this remark. Those papers, in which the Chevalier McArone records his own exploits and reflections, aim to excite mirth by their perfectly preposterous absurdity. (I except, of course, those written toward the close of the author's life, which are inexpressibly pathetic.) Yet, beneath their sunny vein of nonsense, runs an often perceptible current of strong thought and delicate sentiment, revealing the profound convictions and ardent, persuasive sympathy of a great nature. Similar indications appear in his stories. The Poems — of which this volume contains a selection, made and arranged by the present writer — reveal their author yet more distinctly. A subtle knowledge of the human heart, a quick sympathy with ideals of purity, innocence, and beauty, a thorough love for nature, combined with real knowledge of the subject, — in reference to which many poets manifest laborious ignorance, — a fine appreciation of the holiest human emotions, a profound acquaintance with grief, an exhaustless impulse of tender humanity underlying the workings of a critical intellect, a sad, playful humor closely blended with pathos, a vein of religious sentiment, a manly spirit, proud and aspiring, yet capable of calm endurance and gentle resignation, — these qualities of mind and of character are clearly manifested in these poems, which are, moreover, with scarcely an exception, moulded and finished in deference to the dictates of thoughtful culture and severe taste. They do not attempt high, imaginative flights. Their conception was due to no merely artistic plan. They were born in the writer's heart, and uttered naturally, in strains of simple and delicious music.

It does not seem necessary here to enumerate the various magazines and newspapers in which Arnold's pen found employment. He wrote for bread, and he sold his writings to whomsoever would buy them. It was noticeable, too, — especially so in his last years,— that he had no desire for literary reputation. He was industrious, in order that he might be independent of the world. He lived simply, because he could not afford to live magnificently. A poet, he was not lacking in luxurious and eccentric tastes. A young bachelor, he was not lacking in the careless liberality of jovial good-fellowship. Yet he accomplished much work, and he always did it promptly, faithfully, and well. In this respect, and, indeed, in all respects, his private life was governed by the strictest principles of personal integrity. He had, despite his youth, a wide knowledge of the world, and he wisely chose to conquer his place in it, by ability, industry, honor, and cheerfulness. The principal motive of his conduct (and this, possibly, explains his indifference toward literary reputation, and his habitual neglect of the expedients by which commonly it is attained) was a desire to be, rath-

er than to seem, — to develop his own character,
to act ingenuously, to deserve the love of his
friends, to surround himself with an atmosphere
of cheerfulness, and thus to make the best of the
serio-comic drama of human life. In this he suc-
ceeded. Those who knew him well, loved him
dearly. They knew that he was genuine, that he
scorned every description of imposture, and that
his friendship — never idly bestowed — was, when
once given, steadfast and true, alike in storm and
sunshine.

This genuineness of character, revealed through
the medium of a peculiarly cheerful temperament,
—all the more winning for its latent sadness, —
was the source of his peculiar personal influence,
and of his capacity to inspire affection. He
attracted the good side of every nature. Those
who came in contact with him somehow ex-
hibited themselves to the best advantage. He
had no conceit of intellectual superiority,
neither did he flourish his quill in the face of
society. His manners had the repose that dis-

tinguishes the gentleman, and something of the autumnal ripeness and beauty which he so much loved in nature, and of which he has written so well. Even his little superficial affectations were not unpleasant. He was fond of representing himself as an utterly selfish and heartless man, and of attributing selfish motives to the whole human race. He liked, also, to suggest the ludicrous side of serious subjects, and to dampen the fire of sentiment with the cold water of cynicism. But he wore the mask of Mephistopheles with an ill grace, and, toward the last, he laid it altogether aside. Gentle, simple, and affectionate, "a soul of God's best earthly mould," — such he appeared to me, in those last days, and such I faithfully believe him to have been.

It is pleasant to remember that the closing days of his life were passed in the society of dear friends, and that he entered into his rest amidst scenes that were hallowed to him by tender associations of a happy and hopeful youth. His custom, for years, had been to spend occasional weeks of the summer and autumn at Strawberry Farms. Thither, accordingly, he went, in August, 1865, having been ill for some time. His face, though it wore then a weary look, gave no sign of approaching death. Yet his thoughts had dwelt often upon that solemn theme, and I think he knew that the end was near. In spite, however, of sickness, pain, and despondency, his habitual mood of mind remained calm, and even cheerful. He continued to write for the press up to within four weeks of his death. The last prose article that he wrote was the last of the McArone papers, humorously yet very sadly expressive of a wish to be an Old Lady. The last poem that he prepared for publication was "The Matron Year." His final poem was "In the Dark," which ends this volume. Toward the last, however, he used to amuse himself by writing songs, — careless lyrics, not intended for publication. He had a happy aptitude for composing melodies to match his words, and, in private, he used often to sing his own songs.

They were simple and sweet, and he sang them sweetly. Many an afternoon, in that golden autumn which was his last on earth, he sat alone in the parlor of the old house at Strawberry Farms, playing the piano and singing softly to himself. I picture him thus, as the end drew near, — his handsome face calm with the repose of resignation, his gentle, blue eyes full of a kind, sad light, his rich voice, soft, tremulous, and low, breathing out his own glad hymn of faith in the protecting love of the Great Master:

> "To-day a song is on my lips:
> Earth seems a paradise to me:
> For God is good, and lo! my ships
> Are coming home from sea."

They have come home now — all the high hopes, all the ventures of aspiration, that his soul sent forth, in the holy season of innocent youth. His dreams of happiness are all realized: his life that was broken on earth is fulfilled in heaven.

W. W.

New York, January 21, 1866.

PREFACE

POEMS GRAVE AND GAY.

(1867.)

IN the biographical sketch of George Arnold that is prefixed to "Drift" I have recorded the principal events of his life, and have described his character as it was known to me. In that volume, also, I have presented poems which illustrate the nobleness, the gentle simplicity, the tender human sentiment, the winning quaintness, and the half-cheerful, half-sad repose, that were blended in his character, and that made him delightful and dear to his numerous friends. While interpreting his nature, those poems likewise prove his genius. That genius, however, was manifested in various aspects, by other works; and these — in pursuance of the solemn duty that has been intrusted to my hands by the relatives of the departed poet — I am to place before the public. The present volume comprises a number of his poems that have been gathered since the compilation of " Drift," together with a portion of his humorous and satirical verse. There remain to be reproduced his humorous prose writings, his tales and sketches, and those pieces of his comic verse for which he made drawings, and which would lose much of their significance if printed apart from the illustrations. Meanwhile, upon this volume and its predecessor rests George Arnold's title to an honorable fame among the poets of America.

That such a fame awaits him I cannot doubt. To contemplate these poems with the eyes of affection is, perhaps, to see in them a deeper meaning and a higher value than they possess. Yet affection, though it be not critical, is clear-sighted. In this instance, anticipating the verdict of the impartial future, I believe that Arnold will be recognized as truly a poet, — as one, that is, who knew, and worshipped, and could interpret the beautiful; who understood, by poetic intuition, the heart of man and the sanctity of nature; who felt, therefore, the deep, latent tragedy of human life, and heard the voice of God in rustling leaf, and babbling brook, and murmuring surges of ocean; who widely sympathized with the aspirations of humanity, desiring that happiness might prevail as the fruit of justice; who uttered, in admirable forms of art, the truth which he saw and felt, and the ideal for which he longed: and who preserved, through care, and sin, and sorrow, a simple nature, a true heart, and perfect faith in goodness and beauty. This is the testimony of his poems. They do not, indeed, strikingly evince that greatest of poetic faculties, imagination. They do not evince a fixed and controlling intellectual purpose. But they reveal, with vivid clearness, one of those finely organized natures, — seldom sent on earth, but always sent to bless, — in which the fire that burns with such strange, erratic lustre is the divine fire of genius.

It is generally futile to conjecture what a man would have been, and what he would have done, under other circumstances than those which actually surrounded him. Yet I cannot but think — remembering how much greater Arnold was than the writings which he has left — that, under happier conditions, he would have wrought to better purpose and would have enriched the literature of his country with riper and more massive works. The critic will detect in his poetry the elements of fever, recklessness, and melancholy : but it is easy to explain their presence. He lived, ripened, and died within the brief period of thirty-one years. His lot was cast amidst a civilization the enormous physical activity of which precludes repose, and is thus an enemy to genius and to art. Moreover, the best years of his life — which were the last — were those wild years of civil war that forbade poetic meditation. Then, too, his personal experience had warped him from happiness. He began life with exultant enthusiasm. He believed in everything, — in love, in hope, in ambition, in pleasure, in the rewards of the world and in the promises of fame. Passion came to him, and sorrow in its train; but, to his deep nature, a common grief broadened into a profound tragedy. Too brilliant to brood, he plunged into pleasure. Then came a mood of philosophical apathy, in which he tired of love, and sorrow, and the whole strange pageant of human life. Four lines in this book, entitled "An Autobiography," suggest this mood in a forcible manner. Among the last words that he wrote, also, are these, which I copy from the manuscript of his last McArone letter: "To sit in the chimney-corner and smoke a pipe, looking tranquilly backward upon all the troubles, and trials, and tribulations, the losses, the disappointments, the doubtings and fearings that make up the bitterness of life, — to look back upon these as things of the past, matters of history, already uninterest-

ing to the present generation, is a boon I do
mightily desire." In the sad sincerity of these
words his temperament is clearly revealed, — a
temperament that could not, and did not, favor
elaborate efforts in literary art. He wrote continually, however, and without artifice ; and, despite this inward apathy, he never lost the poet's
devotion to nature, nor the gentleman's humane
sensibility, nor the practical thinker's capacity
to cope with the affairs of every-day life. His
sadness was for himself; his cheerfulness was
for others. Those who met George Arnold saw
a handsome, merry creature, whose blue eyes
sparkled with mirth, whose voice was cheerful,
whose manners were buoyant and winning,
whose courtesy was free and gay. He had a
smile and a kind word for every good fellow.
He saw the best side of persons and of things.
His large humanity was quick to find excuses
for the errors and the faults of others. He
could throw himself with hearty zest into
the pleasures of the passing hour ; and thus,

wherever he went, he attracted friends. Among men of letters his presence was sunshine. None could take keener delight than he did in

> "Genial table-talk,
> Or deep dispute and graceful jest."

He mingled with many classes of persons, and he was a favorite with them all. Upon the minds of conventional people, indeed, I dare say that he often left an erroneous impression; for he had a lively impatience of the commonplace in life and letters, and he was remarkably proficient in the art of "chaffing." It is not to be denied, either, that the moral discipline of his life was imperfect. Yet his nature was goodness, and the current of his life sparkled with graces as it flowed onward from light to darkness.

Many pictures of him rise before me, as I think of pleasant hours passed in his society, in years that are forever gone, — of long rambles by day, and sad or merry talk by night, over pipe and bottle, in quiet lodgings wherein we dwelt together.

His affectionate sympathy, his quaint cynicism, his
wit, and his humorous philosophy were, at such
times, inexpressibly winning. He had read many
books, but he had studied man and nature
with deeper relish ; and hence his conversation
was vital and various with the fruits of observa-
tion rather than reading. But no personal rem-
iniscence, no tender, regretful word, can now
reanimate his silent face or rekindle his "spell
o'er hearts." In the love of his friends he can
live but for them alone. For others he must
live in his works, if he live at all.

> "Thy leaf has perished in the green :
>   And, while we breathe beneath the sun,
>   The world, which credits what is done,   .
> Is cold to all that might have been."

What, then, is done? . . . The question is
partly answered in these two volumes of poems.
A few words relative to the details of Arnold's
literary career may chance to answer it still further.

He was a writer from the first. While yet a boy he used to amuse himself by making little newspapers, writing the articles and printing them with his pen. Several years later he began to keep a poetical Diary, in that delicious Italian stanza which probably Byron's " Don Juan " had commended to his fancy. This Diary he kept for a long time, so that it filled a large volume ; but, ultimately, and no doubt wisely, he destroyed it. In letters to his friends, also, — which he used to ornament with illustrative drawings, — his literary faculty found practice. How he drifted from painting to literature, in or about the year 1853, has already been noted. There were fewer periodicals published in New York then than there are now, and hence fewer opportunities were afforded to writers. Yet he was soon actively employed as the sub-editor of a story-paper ; and he was remarkably efficient and successful in this office. His taste, however, soon impelled him to decline editorial cares ; and from this time forward he seldom accepted duties that could restrict his personal freedom.   He could work in the most orderly manner, and with unflagging industry ; but he preferred to work whenever and wherever impulse directed him.   In pursuing this policy he became a contributor to many publications.   His writings, as far as collected, have been drawn from twenty-seven periodicals.   He preserved printed copies of a part of them, but in general was careless of their fate.   The collection of his stories numbers one hundred and ninety-four, and is still incomplete.   To trace all his essays, sketches, art-critiques, book-reviews, jokes, and paragraphs would be impossible, they are so numerous and so widely scattered.   It is enough to say, that many a brilliant article that has anonymously gone the rounds of the press within the last ten years, pleasing hundreds of readers, came from his pen, — carelessly sold, to supply the need of the moment, and then forgotten.   In the prominent magazines of the country he is represented by only a few poems and stories.   He was not fastidious in the sale of his writings.   The nearest purchaser satisfied him. He sometimes gave poems to editors who were his personal friends. He was not, however, a voluminous writer of serious verse. His comic verses are very numerous. At an early period of his literary career he began to write for the comic papers ; and he continued to work in that vein till the end. *Vanity Fair,* which was started in New York in the autumn of 1859, by Mr. W. A. Stephens, gave him constant employ-ment. This paper was discontinued in the sum-mer of 1863, and its record of contributors and contributions has since been partly destroyed ; so that a complete list of the articles that Arnold wrote for it cannot be obtained. But it is certain that he contributed several hundred articles, in prose and verse, many of which he illustrated with pen-and-ink sketches. For *Mrs. Grundy* — com-menced in New York by Dr. A. L. Carroll, in July, 1865, and discontinued after the publication of twelve numbers — he wrote twenty-nine arti-cles, and supplied many clever drawings. His best known efforts in comic writing are his

McArone Letters, commenced in *Vanity Fair*, November 24, 1860, and concluded in the New York *Weekly Review*, October 14, 1865. These letters include a comic novel, in ten chapters. He employed, also, among others, the pen-names of "Grahame Allen," "George Garrulous," " Pierrot," and "The Undersigned."

Other details might be given, but the record of his literary life is sufficiently complete. It was industrious ; it was successful ; it was brilliant : future criticism must finally determine the value of its achievements.

The humorous and satirical poems contained in this volume are mainly those which seem to me to possess a general rather than a merely local and ephemeral interest. Arnold wrote many clever verses in satire of passing events; but, now that the events have passed and been forgotten, the verses would appear to be pointless, if reproduced.

The present collection of serious poems includes, as already intimated, several which I was not able to obtain, prior to the publication of

" Drift," as also several which, at first, I hesitated to print. It is easy to publish ; it is hard to recall. My design has been to allow a genius prematurely broken to express itself in crude and careless suggestion as well as in rounded and adequate utterance. The fact that George Arnold died young, and left his work unfinished, seems to justify the preservation of some pieces which might properly have been rejected had his powers and his labors attained full maturity and scope. The fruits of a poetic mind that is early extinguished by death are entitled to consideration as relics not less than as works of art.

W. W.

New York, August 25, 1866.

NOTE.

This edition of George Arnold's Poems is printed from revised plates. A few slight changes have been made in the editor's preliminary remarks; the poem called " The Old Ramble" and the verses on Patti and Piccolomini, as also a Serenade, have been added; and a few of the lighter verses — having a merely local and temporary drift — have been discarded. It is thought that these alterations have improved the book.

W. W.

Palinode.

I.

Athwart the West, where dies the day,
  A stormy rack of cloud is drifting,
And round the uplands bleak and gray
  The wind its mournful voice is lifting;
With weary moan it says to me
"'Tis night, but She comes not to thee!"

II.

Sharp thorns now grimly deck the bough
  Where clustered once the crimson roses;
With roses once She wreathed this brow
  Where now a thorny crown reposes;
A bitter past alone I see ...
Ah Heaven! She comes no more to me!

———— ❀ ————

The Tryst.

By George Arnold.

I.

On speary grass and starry bloom
  The tiny globes of dew are lying;
The broad moon rises through the gloom
  Of twilight haze; and nightwinds, sighing
In long-drawn whispers, say to me
"'Tis eventide ... She comes to thee!"

II.

A heavy fragrance floods the air
  Where crimson roses climb and cluster.
Heaven seems more near, and Earth more fair...
  The broad moon shines with holier lustre...
A white robe through the dusk I see ...
O, joy, O, Love! She comes to me!

DRIFT, AND OTHER POEMS.

(1866.)

DRIFT.

A SEA-SHORE IDYL.

i.

I WEARIED once of inland fields and hills,
  Of low-lying meadows and of sluggish streams,
Creeping beneath the trees that summer-heats
Had parched to dusty dryness ; and a dream
Of fresh, cool breezes and of salty waves,
Of azure skies o'erarching azure seas,
Of tangled seaweed from unfathomed deeps,
Came over me ; and so I left the hills,
To sojourn, through the riper summer-months,
Upon the shore.

      There, in a lonely house,
So near the breakers that their misty foam
Whitely enwrapped it when the storm raged high,

I let my summer-days pass idly on.
Yet not all idly : when the morn was fair,
And soft winds bore strange odors from the sea
Through open casements, oftentimes I wrote —
Weaving brief rhymes, disjointed, and, perhaps,
Too simple for the lovers of great poems.

A ship went sailing from the shore,
   And vanished in the gleaming west,
Where purple clouds a lining bore
   Of gold and amethyst.

Poised in the air, a sea-gull flashed
   His white wings in the sun's last ray ;
A moment hung, then downward dashed,
   To revel in the spray.

The fishers drew their long nets in
   With careful eye and steady hand,
Till olive back and silvery fin
   Strewed all the tawny sand.

Again I trod the shore ; again
   The sea-gull circled high in air ;
Again the sturdy fishermen
   Drew in their nets with care.

The sunset's gold and amethyst
   Shone fairly, as I paced the shore,
But back from out the gleaming west
   The ship came — nevermore !

II.

After the first days, goodly company
Came to the lonely house beside the sea :
Bright eyes and tresses, voices of young girls,
Made joy within those somewhat mouldy halls ;
And a piano, that had long stood mute
In the old parlor, on the landward side,
Grew musical and merry to the touch
Of jewelled fingers.

              What rare days were those,
When my chief duty was to write a song,
As often as the brown-eyed Marian

Grew weary of my last!   And thus our time
Passed, smoothly as a river-current flows.
Music and reading, strolling on the beach,
Gathering colored pebble-stones and shells,
And sea-weed from the rocks beyond the bar,
Were all our pastime.

A flood of sunlight through a rift
    Between two mounds of yellow sand;
Three sea-gulls on a bit of drift
    Slow surging inward toward the land:

An old dumb-beacon, all awry,
    With drabbled sea-weed round its feet;
A star-like sail against the sky,
    Where sapphire heaven and ocean meet:

This, with the waters swirling o'er
    A shifting stretch of sand and shell,
Will make, for him who loves the shore,
    A picture that may please him well.

III.

Ere the sun went down
We mostly loved to linger by the sea,
Where, seated on some wave-worn slab of stone,
We watched the furrowed waves that rose and fell,
Chasing each other down the beaten strand ;
But when the shadows lengthened toward the east,
And the red glory of the sunset shone
Upon the light-house, and the fading sails,
The yellow sand-hills with their sickly grass
And inland-leaning cedars, we returned
To the old parlor ; and, as dusk came on,
Sang to each other till the moon rode high.

The light-house keeper's daughter, —
Her hair is golden as the sand ;
Her eyes are blue as summer-seas
That melt into the land.

Her brow and neck are whiter
Than sea-foam flying on the wind,
Her mouth is rosy as the shells
That strew the coast of Ind.

The winds caress her ringlets
　That down her neck in clusters stray,
And frothy waves flow tenderly
　About her feet, in play.

I love this simple maiden,
　She grows upon me more and more,
And — ask the moon who 't was that kissed,
　Last night, upon the shore !

IV.

At times, when moonlight danced upon the sea,
And all the air was musical with sounds
Of waters slowly breaking on the beach,
We sought the bar, and climbed its furthest rocks,
Against whose weedy feet the waves uprose
In phosphorescent foam ; and, seated there,
The maidens picturesquely grouped around,
We talked philosophy, or told quaint tales
Of most romantic sort, — of ghosts and ghouls,
Of strange things seen by those whom we had
　　known ;

Of strange things we, perchance, ourselves had
    seen ;
Of marvels told by ancient mariners,
The Maelstrom, and the heaven-dropped water-
    spouts, —
Or sadder tales, of wrecks far out at sea,
Of missing vessels, and of sailors drowned.

  The river down to the ocean flows
    By reedy flats and marshes bare ;
  And the leafless poplars stand in rows
    Like ghostly sentinels watching there.

  An osprey sails, with wings spread wide,
    Down-slanting from his even flight,
  To a sedgy spot, where the falling tide
    Has left some kind of drift in sight.

  A blackened mass, by the tide left bare,
    In the tangled weeds and the slimy mud.
  The osprey shrieks as he settles there,
    And a deathly horror chills my blood !

v.

So passed the summer, and we had our fill
Of lotos-eating by the ocean side ;
We came to know and love each pleasant spot
About the place ; the sheltered nooks where grew
Dwarfed flowers, whose downy seeds had come,
          mayhap,
Upon the wings of autumn's winds upborne,
A thousand miles, to drop, and germinate,
In the dry sand ; to grow, and blow, and bloom,
And then to wither — 't were a happy fate —
In brown-eyed Marian's bosom.   And we knew
Each craggy rock that overhung the sea,
Whence we could gaze far out across the waste
Of heaving waters, dotted here and there
With sails that shone and glimmered in the sun,
Like planets in a mellow evening sky.
Sometimes we went adventurously forth
When northeast tempests raged along the coast,
Flinging the white foam upward in great sheets,
Like hungry monsters rushing from the deep
To swallow up the land.

Then, bits of wrecks,
Odd timbers spiked with rusty iron bolts,
Fragments of masts, and empty water-casks, —
Sad débris of the storm, — came up next day,
Drifting ashore on smooth, unbroken swells.

O cool, green waves that ebb and flow,
    Reflecting calm, blue skies above,
How gently now ye come and go,
    Since ye have drowned my' love !

Ye lap the shore of beaten sand,
    With cool, salt ripples circling by ;
But from your depths a ghostly hand
    Pcints upward to the sky.

O waves ! strew corals, white and red,
    With shells and strange weeds from the deep,
To make a rare and regal bed
    Whereon my love may sleep :

May sleep, and, sleeping, dream of me,
    In dreams that lovers find so sweet ;

And I will couch me by the sea,
    That we in dreams may meet.

VI.

But, while the pleasant season lasted still,
My friends deserted me for other scenes,
Leaving me lonely in the lonely house,
With memory's ghosts to bear me company.
Alone I sang the plaintive little songs,
That brown-eyed Marian had sung with me :
Alone I trod the path along the shore,
Where we so often had together strolled :
Alone I watched the moonrise, from the rocks
Where Marian had erstwhile walked with me,
To let the salt breeze, freshening with the night,
Play in her ringlets, and bring up the bloom
Of rose and lily to her cheek.
                                    Alas !
If I should tell the whole of what I felt,
In waking these dear memories of the past,
This simple idyl would be lengthened out
Into a history of two hearts, that met —
That met — and parted !

     Ah ! the theme is old,
And worn quite threadbare, — not alone in books,
But in the hearts of men and maids as well.
But then, all stories that are true are old.

The breakers come and the breakers go,
  Along the silvery sand,
With a changing line of feathery snow,
  Between the water and land.

Sea-weeds gleam in the sunset light,
  On the ledges of wave-worn stone ;
Orange and crimson, purple and white,
  In regular windrows strewn.

The waves grow calm in the dusk of eve,
  When the wind goes down with the sun ;
So fade the smiles of those who deceive,
  When the coveted heart is won.

This seaweed wreath that hangs on the wall,
  She twined one day by the sea :
Of the weeds, and the waves, and her love, it is all
  That the Past has left to me !

THE JOLLY OLD PEDAGOGUE.

I.

'T WAS a jolly old pedagogue, long ago,
   Tall and slender, and sallow and dry ;
His form was bent, and his gait was slow,
His long, thin hair was as white as snow,
   But a wonderful twinkle shone in his eye ;
And he sang every night as he went to bed,
   " Let us be happy down here below ;
The living should live, though the dead be dead,"
   Said the jolly old pedagogue, long ago.

II.

He taught his scholars the rule of three,
   Writing, and reading, and history, too ;
He took the little ones up on his knee,
For a kind old heart in his breast had he,
   And the wants of the littlest child he knew :

" Learn while you 're young," he often said,
  " There is much to enjoy, down here below ;
Life for the living, and rest for the dead ! "
  Said the jolly old pedagogue, long ago.

III.

With the stupidest boys he was kind and cool,
  Speaking only in gentlest tones ;
The rod was hardly known in his school...
Whipping, to him, was a barbarous rule,
  And too hard work for his poor old bones ;
Beside, it was painful, he sometimes said :
  "We should make life pleasant, down here below,
The living need charity more than the dead,"
  Said the jolly old pedagogue, long ago.

IV.

He lived in the house by the hawthorn lane,
  With roses and woodbine over the door ;
His rooms were quiet, and neat, and plain,
But a spirit of comfort there held reign,
  And made him forget he was old and poor ;

" I need so little," he often said ;
  " And my friends and relatives here below
Won't litigate over me when I am dead,"
  Said the jolly old pedagogue, long ago.

V.

But the pleasantest times that he had, of all,
  Were the sociable hours he used to pass,
With his chair tipped back to a neighbor's wall,
Making an unceremonious call,
  Over a pipe and a friendly glass :
This was the finest pleasure, he said,
  Of the many he tasted, here below ;
" Who has no cronies, had better be dead !"
  Said the jolly old pedagogue, long ago.

VI.

Then the jolly old pedagogue's wrinkled face
  Melted all over in sunshiny smiles ;
He stirred his glass with an old-school grace,
Chuckled, and sipped, and prattled apace,
  Till the house grew merry, from cellar to tiles :

"I 'm a pretty old man," he gently said,
  " I have lingered a long while, here below ;
But my heart is fresh, if my youth is fled !"
  Said the jolly old pedagogue, long ago.

VII.

He smoked his pipe in the balmy air,
  Every night when the sun went down,
While the soft wind played in his silvery hair,
Leaving its tenderest kisses there,
  On the jolly old pedagogue's jolly old crown :
And, feeling the kisses, he smiled, and said,
  'T was a glorious world, down here below ;
" Why wait for happiness till we are dead ?"
  Said the jolly old pedagogue, long ago.

VIII.

He sat at his door, one midsummer night,
  After the sun had sunk in the west,
And the lingering beams of golden light
Made his kindly old face look warm and bright,
  While the odorous night-wind whispered, " Rest !"

Gently, gently, he bowed his head . . .
　　There were angels waiting for him, I know ;
He was sure of happiness, living or dead,
　　This jolly old pedagogue, long ago !

RECRIMINATION.

I.

THE prime of summer is coming, and with it
there comes, to-day,
A thought of another summer, whose garlands
have faded away.
The tall laburnums are covered with tresses of
yellow flowers,
As they were when under their shadow you used
to loiter for hours;
And the blackberry's starry blossom and the
buttercup's chalice of gold
Bloom bright in the ancient forest where you
loved to wander of old, —
Where you loved to wander at even, but wan-
dered never alone;
For a manly form was beside you, and a voice of
manly tone

Told ever the olden story; the tale that you know
　　so well,
You seem to think it the only one it is worth
　　man's while to tell.
Come, sit you down here and listen; I have many
　　things to say,
And though I am loath to blame you, yet pity I
　　surely may.

II.

Ay, ay, you wince!　I fancy you would rather have
　　blame instead.
O girl! will you never learn wisdom?　I had
　　hoped your pride was dead;
But no,—it will last and flourish so long as vani-
　　ties live,—
So long as you hunger for worship, so long as
　　your subjects give.
It was strange that he thought you loved him; it
　　was strange that he never knew
Your heart, except by the shadow that others
　　mistook for you:

But you went well masked, and no one, whether
    you laughed or wept,
Knew aught of the secret chamber where your
    broken relics were kept ;
You hid them so very securely the wisest had
    hardly guessed,
From your light-hearted tone and manner, your
    outer seeming of rest,
That your heart was a drear Golgotha, where all
    the ground was white
With the wrecks of joys that had perished, — the
    skeletons of delight !

III.

He loved you ; his soul was in earnest ; at your
    dainty feet he poured
The purest and best libation that human hearts
    can afford :
He dreamed of you morn and even ; he cherished
    the flowers you gave ;
And I tell you, though they are withered now,
    they will go with him to the grave !

But you — how was it ? — you met him with
    marvellous glances and smiles ;
You wove your glittering meshes ; you compassed
    him with your wiles ;
You sang the songs he had written ; you talked
    in your sweetest voice,
Till he thought his bondage was freedom, and
    wore your fetters by choice.
Then a great joy flooded his spirit, and the yellow
    laburnum flowers
Heard wondrous vows and pledges, in the dusk of
    the evening hours ;
While there, in your heart, close hidden with jeal-
    ously watchful care,
Lay that strange Golgotha of passion, that arid
    waste of despair !

IV.

It is well that I know your story : I know that
    your first love came,
As of old came Jove to Semele, a splendid and
    fatal flame :

And it left your heart in ashes, — dead ashes, that
    cooled and lay
A wearisome weight in your bosom, a burden to
    bear for aye.
Since then you have shown no mercy to any that
    circle around
The dangerous blaze of your beauty, for you no
    mercy had found.
Tis for this I offer you pity, and blame you not,
    as I should
Had you still a heart that was human, with a
    human knowledge of good ;
But the glass of your life is darkened, and darkly
    through it you see
Distorted and ghastly fragments of duty and des-
    tiny.
Yet you still can flirt and trifle, still live in folly
    and mirth, —
Ah ! they say that revenge is sweeter than any-
    thing else on earth.

v.

But are there no better moments — better? or
    are they worse ? —
When flattery loses its sweetness, and beauty
    becomes a curse ?
When you come from the world of pleasure, the
    whirl, and glitter, and glare,
The tattle instead of wisdom, the perfume instead
    of air ;
When the hot-house garlands are withered, and
    the gray dawn breaks in the east,
And the wine grows stale in the goblets that
    shone so fair at the feast ;
When rouge hides paleness no longer, and folly
    gives way to thought, —
Do love, and life, and emotion still count in your
    creed for naught ?
Do you never gaze in your mirror, when your
    beauty at daybreak goes,
And, pressing your throbbing temples, pray God
    to give you repose ?

Repose! it is tardy in coming: when the bitter
    chalice is filled,
We must wait till the feverish pulses and the
    passionate heart are stilled.

VI.

There is one, that we know, thus waiting, — wait-
    ing and thinking to-day,
Perchance, of the happy summer whose blossoms
    have faded away:
He walks beneath the laburnums, but not with
    the hopeful pride
That made his world such an Eden when you
    walked there by his side.
O love! 't is a wonderful passion; it makes or it
    mars us all;
By love men may walk with the angels, by love
    the angels may fall!
And you — it has changed your nature, it has
    warped you, heart and soul,
Till you flee, with fierce desperation, the genii
    you cannot control.

What, tears ? they are not becoming ; let others
　　such weakness show, —
The hall is garnished for dancing, the wine and
　　the gaslights glow :
Go, stifle your sobs with laughter, let your eyes,
　　like your heart, be dry,
And pray, when the ball is over, to be forgiven —
　　and die !

INTROSPECTION.

I.

HAVE you sent her back her letters? have
    you given her back her ring?
Have you tried to forget the haunting songs that
    you loved to hear her sing?
Have you cursed the day you met her first?
    thanked God that you were free,
And said in your inmost heart, as you thought,
    "She never was dear to me"?
You have cast her off; your pride is touched;
    you fancy that all is done;
That for you the world is bright again, and
    bravely shines the sun:
You have washed your hands of passion; you
    have whistled her down the wind, —
O Tom, old friend, this goes before, the sharpest
    comes behind!

Yes, the sharpest is yet to come, for love is a
　　　plant that never dies;
Its roots are deep as the earth itself, its branches
　　　wide as the skies;
And wherever once it has taken hold, it flourishes
　　　evermore,
Bearing a fruit that is fair outside, but bitter
　　　ashes at core.

II.

You will learn this, Tom, hereafter, when anger
　　　has cooled, and you
Have time for introspection; you will find my
　　　words are true;
You will sit and gaze in your fire alone, and fancy
　　　that you can see
Her face, with its classic oval, her ringlets flutter-
　　　ing free,
Her soft blue eyes, wide opened, her sweet red
　　　lips apart,
As she used to look, in the golden days when you
　　　fancied she had a heart:

Whatever you do, wherever you turn, you will see
    that glorious face
Coming with shadowy beauty, to haunt all time
    and space :
Those songs you wrote for her singing will sing
    themselves into your brain
Till your life seems set to their rhythm, and your
    thoughts to their refrain —
Their old, old burden of love and grief — the
    passion you have forsworn :
I tell you, Tom, it is not thrown off so well as
    you think, this morn !

III.

But the worst, perhaps the worst of all, will be
    when the day has flown,
When darkness favors reflection, and your com-
    rades leave you alone :
You will try to sleep, but the memories of unfor-
    gotten years
Will come with a storm of wild regret — mayhap
    with a storm of tears ;

Each 'look, each word, each playful tone, each
    timid little caress,
The golden gleam of her ringlets, the rustling of
    her dress,
The delicate touch of her ungloved hand, that
    woke such an exquisite thrill,
The flowers she gave you, the night of the ball, —
    I think you treasure them still, —
All these will come, till you slumber, worn out by
    sheer despair,
And then you will hear vague echoes of song on
    the darkened air, —
Vague echoes, rising and falling, of the voice you
    know so well,
Like the songs that were sung by the Lurlei-
    maids, sweet with a deadly spell !

IV.

In dreams, her heart will ever again be yours, and
    you will see
Fair glimpses of what might have been, — what
    now can never be ;

And as she comes to meet you, with a sudden
    wild unrest
You stretch your arms forth lovingly, to fold her
    to your breast :
But the Lurlei-song will faint and die, and with
    its fading tone
You wake to find you clasp the thin and empty
    air alone,
While the fire-bell's clanging dissonance, on the
    gusty night-wind borne
Will seem an iron-tongued demon's voice, laugh-
    ing your grief to scorn.
O Tom, you say it is over, — you talk of letters
    and rings, —
Do you think that love's mighty spirit, then, is
    held by such trifling things ?
No ! if you once have truly loved, you will still
    love on, I know,
Till the churchyard myrtles blossom above, and
    you lie mute below !

v.

How is it, I wonder, hereafter ?   Faith teaches us
     little, here,
Of the ones we have loved and lost on earth, — do
     you think they will still be dear ?
Shall we live the lives we might have led ? — will
     those who are severed now
Remember the pledge of a lower sphere, and re-
     new the broken vow ?
It almost drives me wild to think of the gifts we
     throw away
Unthinking whether or no we lose life's honey
     and wine for aye !
But then, again, 't is a mighty joy — greater than
     I can tell —
To trust that the parted may some time meet, —
     that all may again be well :
However it be, I hold that all the evil we know
     on earth
Finds in this violence done to love its true and
     legitimate birth,

And the agonies we suffer, when the heart is left
    alone,
For every sin of humanity should fully and well
    atone !

VI.

I see that you marvel greatly, Tom, to hear such
    words from me,
But, if you knew my inmost heart, 't would be no
    mystery.
Experience is bitter, but its teachings we retain ;
It has taught me this,—who once has loved, loves
    never on earth again !
And I, too, have my closet, with a ghastly form
    inside, —
The skeleton of a perished love, killed by a cruel
    pride :
I sit by the fire at evening, as you will some time
    sit,
And watch, in the roseate half-light, the ghosts of
    happiness flit :

I, too, awaken at midnight, and stretch my arms
  to enfold
A vague and shadowy image, with tresses of
  brown and gold:
Experience is bitter indeed, — I have learned at a
  heavy cost
The secret of love's persistency: I, too, have
  loved and lost!

WOOL-GATHERING.

I.

A PLEASANT golden light fills all the chamber where I sit,
The amber curtains close are drawn, and shadows
o'er them flit, —
The swaying, shifting shadows of the honeysuckle
vine,
Whose bare and leafless branches still about the
porch entwine :
In summer, fresh and fair they grow, with blossoms for the bees,
But now in wintry nakedness they swing upon the
breeze ;
Yet here, inside, 't is warm and bright, and I am
quite inclined
To let this golden *demi-jour* make summer in my
mind :

I sit with Jack — my terrier-dog — upon my lap
    curled up,
And, smoking thoughtfully, I seem to sip the
    classic cup
The Ancients called Nepenthe, — 't is a draught
    that brings repose
When one has lived or loved too much, — a balm
    for mental woes.
Yet, in this same Nepenthe cup, I know that some
    will see
Another name for laziness, — a common fault with
    me!

II.

Well, why not preach up laziness? I think it
    would be well
If some who cry it down a sin could only feel its
    spell!
The hard, ascetic natures — those who look for
    naught but use
In everything one says or does — whose spirits
    are obtuse

To all the glorious gains of art, to all the joys of
    sense,
And who cut their hard paths straightly by Poor
    Richard's eloquence !
Cui bono? Is there not a Power above the hu-
    man mind
That works out all our problems, be they e'er so
    darkly blind ?
And, after all, does Man, the unit, when his life is
    done
Ever look back upon its field to see the battle
    won ?
No ; I think not : we lay our plans, but when our
    life-star pales
We learn that human prescience inevitably
    fails.
Napoleon on his island, and Columbus in his
    chains, —
Are these the proud successes, then, for which we
    take such pains ?

III.

Ah, many a one has started forth with hope and
    purpose high ;
Has fought throughout a weary life, and passed
    all pleasure by ;
Has burst all flowery chains by which men aye
    have been enthralled ;
Has been stone-deaf to voices sweet, that softly,
    sadly called ;
Has scorned the flashing goblet with the bubbles
    on its brim ;
Has turned his back on jewelled hands that madly
    beckoned him ;
Has, in a word, condemned himself to follow out
    his plan
By stern and lonely labor, — and has died, a con-
    quered man !
Look back, ye men of lofty aims, who in your
    youth aspired
To win some prize, — with love of gold or glory
    ye were fired ;

But now ? let those who count threescore-and-ten
    full circles past
Tell how much they have gained and lost, — how
    much they hold at last !
Napoleon and Columbus, and legions more whose
    names
We never even heard of, — these were men of lofty
    aims !

IV.

So, in this softened, yellow light, with Jack upon
    my knees,
I find my good in being just as lazy as I
    please ;
My pipe-smoke floats aspiringly, and that, I 'm
    fain to say,
Is as much of aspiration as I care to see to-
    day ;
Though Jack, disturbed by canine dreams, gives
    forth a sleepy cry,
And, full of lofty aims, prepares to conquer or to
    die ;

No doubt some mighty, spectral rat glares through
    his visions dim,
Which Jack is bound to vanquish, or the rat will
    vanquish him !
Well, well, my dog, be wise, and all these high am-
    bitions keep ;
Unlike poor man, indulge them only when you are
    asleep ! —
What's this ?   I find that while in praise of lazi-
    ness I sang,
I 've worked quite hard to write a metaphysical
    harangue !
Well, thus it is ; consistency exists on earth no
    more, —
My pipe is out, my dog has waked, my laziness is
    o'er !

THE TWO AUTUMNS.

THE tall grass waves o'er lowly graves,
  The golden sunshine floods the meadows,
    And in the breeze the willow-trees,
    That guard the tomb of Eloise,
Wave to and fro, with flickering shadows.

And here I sit, while bright birds flit
  Among the gravestones whitely gleaming,
    And muse away the summer day
    Beneath the vines' and willows' sway, —
On that fair maiden's memory dreaming.

O'er fields unmown the poppy shone,
The earliest rose had hardly perished,
    When she confessed that in her breast
    Young love was throned, a royal guest, —
My image there alone she cherished.

O happy hour, when from her bower,
With clambering grape-vines close entangled,
We saw the moon of leafy June
Rise calmly o'er the wide lagoon,
And climb the sky with bright stars spangled.

Her deep blue eyes, like tropic skies, —
Not less profound, and never colder, —
Were fixed on mine with gaze divine,
And, golden as the German wine,
Her regal ringlets swept her shoulder.

Her little hand, which scarcely spanned
With timid clasp my first three fingers,
Her lip, her cheek, which bees might seek ;
Her voice — but, ah! mere words are weak
To paint the joys where memory lingers!

The summer passed, and autumn's blast
Swept bleakly cold across the heather ;

The bright leaves browned, 'neath skies that
    frowned,
Then whirled in circles to the ground,
And strewed the paths we trod together.

O heavy grief! with autumn's leaf
They told me that her days were numbered :
    She passed away, — her mortal clay
    In death's pale beauty silent lay,
As calm as if she only slumbered.

I sit among the graves o'erhung
With many a slender-threaded willow;
    The churchyard mould seems now less cold
    Since, deep beneath, those locks of gold
Have found a soft and dreamless pillow.

About the tombs the laurel blooms,
I hear the bees above it humming,
    The zephyrs sigh, in floating by ;
    They bring the scent of ripened rye,
And tell another autumn coming.

Far down upon the horizon
A purple haze is softly falling,
　The fading rose of summer goes,
　And distant bells, at day's repose,
Unto my inner ear are calling.

　Ah, dreamily they say to me
That those, who here are called to sever,
　Are elsewhere blessed with peace and rest,
　And I, unto this lonely breast
Shall clasp my Eloise forever.

ALONE BY THE HEARTH.

H ERE, in my snug little fire-lit chamber,
      Sit I alone ;
And, as I gaze in the coals, I remember
      Days long agone.

Saddening it is, when the night has descended,
      Thus to sit here,
Pensively musing on episodes, ended
      Many a year.

Still in my visions a golden-haired glory
      Floats to and fro ;
She whom I loved, — but 't is just the old story,
      Dead, long ago !

'T is but the wraith of a love; yet I linger
      (Thus passion errs),

Foolishly kissing the ring on my finger,—
    Once it was hers.

Nothing has changed since her spirit departed,
    Here, in this room,
Save I, who, weary and half broken-hearted,
    Sit in the gloom.

Loud 'gainst the window the winter rain dashes,
    Dreary and cold ;
Over the floor the red fire-light flashes
    Just as of old.

Just as of old,—but the embers are scattered,
    Whose ruddy blaze
Flashed o'er the floor where her fairy feet pattered
    In other days !

Then, her dear voice, like a silver-chime ringing,
    Melted away ;
Often these walls have re-echoed her singing
    Now hushed for aye !

Why should love bring naught but sorrow, I won-
der?
Everything dies!
Time and Death, sooner or later, must sunder
Holiest ties.

Years have rolled by; I am wiser and older,—
Wiser, but yet,
Not till my heart and its feelings grow colder,
Can I forget.

So, in my snug little fire-lit chamber,
Sit I alone;
And, as I gaze in the coals, I remember
Days long agone!

THE GARDEN OF MEMORY.

THERE is a garden which my memory knows,
  A grand old garden of the days gone by,
  Where lofty trees invite the breeze,
And underneath them blooms full many a rose,
  Of rarest crimson or deep purple dye ;
And there extend as far as eye can see,
Dim vistas of cool greenery.

Quaint marble statues, clothed with vines and
    mould,
  Gleam gray and spectral 'mid the foliage there:
  Grimly they stand on every hand,
Along the walk whose sands are smoothly rolled
  And borders trimmed with constant, watchful
    care :
There Memory sits, and hears soft voices call
Above the plashing waterfall.

'Old, faded bowers, with their rustic seats
   Of knotted branches closely intertwined,
   May there be seen, the walks between :
Within their shade the dove at noon retreats,
   And gives her sad voice to the summer wind ;
Around them bloom rich flowers, where all day
      long
The wild bee drones his dreamy song.

The garden stretches downward to a lake,
   Where gentle ripples kiss a pebbly shore :
   All cool and deep the waters sleep,
With naught the calm of their repose to break
   Save now and then the plashing of an oar,
Or the long train of diamond sparkles bright
Left by the wayward swallow's flight.

Within that garden Memory oft recalls
   Gay friends, who lived, and loved, and passed
      away :
Who met at morn upon the lawn,

And strolled in couples by the garden-walls,
  Or on the grass beneath the maples lay,
And passed the hours as gayly as might be,
With olden tales of chivalry.

The younger maidens, each with silken net,
    Chased butterflies that hung, on painted wings,
    Above the beds where poppy-heads
Drooped heavily with morning dew-drops wet:
    In recollection still their laughter rings,
And still I seem to see them sport among
The statues gray, with vines o'erhung.

One sainted maiden I remember well,
    And shall remember, though all else should
        fade:
    Her dreamy eyes, her gentle sighs,
Her golden hair in tangled curls that fell,
    Her queen-like beauty and demeanor staid,
And O, her smile, that played at hide-and-seek
With dimples on her chin and cheek!

O Edith! often have we sat at rest,
  And watched the sunset from the Lover's
    Hill,
  When few, faint stars shone through the bars
Of purple cloud that stretched athwart the west;
  And nature's pulse seemed silently to thrill,
While night came o'er the moorlands wide and
    brown,
On dusky pinions sweeping down.

Long years have faded since those happy days,
  Yet still in memory are their joys enshrined.
  Tall grasses wave o'er Edith's grave;
Above her breast the birds sing plaintive lays;
  Yet still I feel her arms about me twined;
Still float her tangled tresses in the breeze;
Still sit we 'neath the maple-trees.

Thus may it be, until I too am gone!
  Thus let me ever dream of youth and love!
  And when the strife of earthly life

Is past ; when all my weary tasks are done,
  I know that in some garden there, above,
My angel Edith waits to welcome me
Unto thy halls, Eternity !

AN IDYL OF OCTOBER.

JULIE, Mary, Willie, and I,
  Walked down the cedar-lane one day,
When the sun was bright in an autumn sky,
  And the trees with their autumn tints were gay ;
Down to the bridge our way we took,
  Past the chestnuts that crown the hill, —
Down to the bridge that crosses the brook,
  On the road to the cider-mill.

A year before, we had trod the lane,
  And then, half-jesting, ourselves we bound
To take the selfsame walk again,
  When another year had rolled around ; —
So, when another October glowed
  On shrubby hollow and wooded ridge,
It found us threading the cedar-road,
  And loitering on the bridge.

The water swirled 'mong the oaken posts,
　　In long, dark currents, eddying by,
And floating leaves, like shadowy ghosts,
　　Were borne on its bosom silently.
The breezes dallied with Julie's hair,
　　Where mingling gold and amber played;
Fair Mary's face seemed still more fair
　　In the flickering shine and shade.

We feasted our eyes on the pleasant scene,
　　We gathered leaves of a thousand dyes,—
Speckled with crimson, spotted with green,
　　And shaded with hues from Paradise;
We sang and shouted, we laughed and talked,
　　Till the woods were loud with our echoed glee;—
O, never a merrier party walked
　　In a place more fair to see!

Last year, when under the autumn sky,
　　Through these bright autumn woods we strolled,
We met a lassie, pretty and shy,
　　Mayhap some seventeen summers old:

A blue-eyed, bashful country maid,
    Who passed us, timidly glancing down,
Her blue eyes taking a deeper shade
    From their lashes long and brown.

I, who have ever been *farceur*, —
    Loving a merry word alway, —
Feigned to have fallen in love with her, —
    A new-born passion, to last for aye.
So, when we spoke of the cedar-lane,
    And plans for this year's ramble laid,
We wondered if we should meet again
    With the blue-eyed, bashful maid.

Then, I said that if we should meet
    With the country lassie, modest and fair,
There on the bridge would I kneel at her feet,
    And all my passion for her declare . . .
Well, as we came to the foot of the hill,
    Where the maples glow like a colored flame,
Down the road to the cider-mill,
    The blue-eyed damsel came !

But, alas for the ways of destiny !
　I spied some leaves so gorgeously hued,
Decking the boughs of a maple-tree,
　By a fence between the road and the wood,
That I vowed to have them whether or no, —
　Coveting beauty as some covet pelf, —
And, venturing where the ground was low,
　In a swamp I found myself.

There I gathered the prettiest leaves,
　Standing, the while, on treacherous ground, —
Such fair chaplets as Nature weaves
　When Autumn, King of the Year, is crowned, —
And there, alone, long after its time,
　I found a heaven-blue violet,
Gleaming up from the ooze and slime
　Like a jewel, foully set.

Many a leaf of orange and red,
　Gold and purple, scarlet and brown,
I found on the branches overhead,
　Or where the wind had rustled them down ;

Gathering these, no heed I paid
  To anything save my leafy load,
And the blue-eyed, bashful country maid
  Had gone, when I gained the road !

But Julie and Mary both were there, —
  Better than bashful maids are they, —
The blue-eyed lassie is not more fair,
  And not more modest, as I dare say ;
I felt some pride, as surely I might,
  When I showed my leaves and my violet ; —
Those autumn colors were wondrous bright,
  But those faces were brighter yet !

Whenever I see those leaves again,
  Pressed and varnished by Julie's skill,
I shall think of our walk in the cedar-lane,
  And the bridge on the road to the cider-mill ;
And if e'er for the bashful lassie I sigh, —
  I, who have ever been *farceur*, —
I will see that she does not pass me by ; —
  I 'll wait on the bridge for her !

"ALL FOR LOVE."

ABOUT the pool the pansies blow,
　　Fair they bloom in the summer sun,
With violets on the bank below
　　And tangled vines that at random run ;
The water is dark, and cool, and green,
　　Its surface touched by misty rays
That slant the willow boughs between
　　On sunny, summer days.

Across the pool the wingéd seeds
　　Hither and thither lightly flaunt,
Blown from the shore of bristling reeds
　　That gauzy dragon-flies love to haunt ;
The shallows all are thickly set
　　With lily-leaves and blossoms white, —
Their fragrant petals glistening wet
　　With dewdrops, diamond-bright.

A silence reigns upon the air,
   Upon the pansies by the shore,
Upon the violets, pale and fair,
   Upon the willow, bending o'er ;
The reeds and lilies silent grow,
   The dark green waters silent sleep,
Save when the summer breezes blow,
   Or silvery minnows leap.

Adown the path, that hidden lies
   Under the chestnuts on the hill,
Came pretty May with the hazel eyes,
   Whose father kept the neighboring mill.
Wild she muttered and long she gazed,
   Loosely floated her fair, brown hair :
Like one by a heavy sorrow crazed
   She laughed and whispered there.

Alas ! her story was just the same
   That poets have told since poets have sung, —
Beginning in love, to end in shame,
   When hope grows old while life is young !

So, sighing wearily, down she strayed,
　　While the sunshine slept on the silent pool,
To the flowery bank, and the willow's shade,
　　And the water, deep and cool.

About the pool the pansies blow,
　　Fair in the summer sun they bloom,
But the water is dark that lies below, —
　　Dark and silent as is the tomb :
And I seem to see, wherever I tread
　　The reedy shore where the willow stands,
The sorrowing wraith of one long dead,
　　Wringing her ghostly hands.

The mill and miller have long been gone,
　　The father sleeps by his daughter's side,
And many a summer's sun has shone
　　Since hazel-eyed May lived, loved, and died ;
Yet still in passing, the neighbors pause,
　　And say, as they glance from the hill above,
" Let us forgive the child, because
　　Her sorrow was born of love ! "

THE BALLAD OF ROSALIE.

ROSALIE was strangely fair
    — Slow and weary the days go by —
With her splendid torrent of tawny hair,
    And her terrible, beautiful eye.

Love for her had made me blind,
    — Slow and weary the days go by —
Her heart was false as the summer wind,
    Her truest truth was a lie.

O, but she vowed by that and by this!
    — Slow and weary the days go by —
O, but her lips were sweet to kiss, .
    And, O, but her heart was dry.

A chaplet once I saw her weave,
    — Slow and weary the days go by —

Her girdle pressed against my sleeve ;
My cheek warmed to her sigh.

That night, wine in the cup was red,
  — Slow and weary the days go by —
The chaplet shone on Rosalie's head,
  So Roland's time drew nigh.

Song and laughter, peal on peal !
  — Slow and weary the days go by —
They could not hear the clash of steel,
  Their merriment rang so high.

Under the trees I left the knight,
  — Slow and weary the days go by --
My blade was crimson ; his face was white ;
  I wear good steel on thigh.

Morning came and the broad light shone,
  — Slow and weary the days go by —
The dancers and revellers all had gone
  When the sun climbed up the sky.

Rosalie lay by the castle moat,
  — Slow and weary the days go by —
A dark, red line across her throat.
  — 'T were pity that she should die!

Her bright hair gleamed by the water-side,
  — Slow and weary the days go by —
How she was loved and how she died
  Nobody knows but I.

TRAILING ARBUTUS.

I.

WANDERING over the breezy slopes
   Where the trailing arbutus grows,
(That little flower that timidly opes,
While the wind of March still blows,
Its delicate buds of the palest rose,
And blossoms white as eternal snows),
O Love, we walked, and cheerily talked,
That breezy, blustering day,
Where the March winds blow, and the pink buds
      grow,
Wet with the morning's crystalline dew;
And far below us, stretching away
'Neath the sky with its spring-time azure hue,
The heaving, flashing, glittering bay
In solemn breadth and beauty lay!

II.

Sitting under the cedar-trees,
Breathing their odor rare,
With the swaying, swinging, dallying breeze
Playing among thy hair,
Ah, still my fancy thy image sees, —
The checkered shadow and shine on thy face,
Lighting the place with a holy grace,
While thy voice was lifted in ballads old
Of maids who were fair, and men who were bold, —
Ah, heaven! thou too wert fair!

III.

The wind is blowing and blustering still
On the lofty cedared slopes,
And still on the southerly face of the hill
The trailing arbutus opes ;
But alone I sit 'neath the cedar-trees, —
Alone with the boisterous, blustering breeze,
The flowers, and my own sad memories ;
While the murmur that comes from the flashing seas
Whispers to me, all solemnly,

That love is only a vanity ! . . .
Well, it has flown, as the winds have blown
Last autumn's dead leaves rustling down.
Each spring, the trailing arbutus grows
When the March wind blows, but love, when it
  goes,
Alas, is forever gone !

THE OLD PLACE.

I STAND on the shore of a moonlit sea,
   Under the stars of a summer sky,
And sad are the thoughts that come to me,
   As the sorrowful night-wind whispers by.

'T is the same old sea whose voices call,
   The same old stars, with their twinkling eyes,
The same old moonlight silvers all,
   And the same old solemn thoughts arise.

Naught in the scene has changed, for years,
   Waves, nor stars, nor moonlight fair ;
And here in my eyes are the same old tears,
   For the same old hopeless love I bear.

THE GIFT OF LOVE.

"GIVE me," I said, "that ring,
  Which on thy taper finger gleams ;
  Sweet thoughts to me 't will bring,
When summer sunset's beams
    Have faded o'er the western sea,
    And left me dreaming, Love, of thee !"

  "O no !" the maiden cried ;
"This shining ring is bright, but cold :
  That bond is loosely tied
Which must be clasped with gold !
    The ring would soon forgotten be :
    Some better gift I 'll give to thee !"

  "Then give me that red rose,"
Said I, "which on thy bosom heaves
  In ecstasied repose,

And droops its blushing leaves :
 If thou wouldst have me think of thee,
 Fair maiden, give the rose to me!"

"O no!" she softly said,
"I will not give thee any flower :
 This rose will surely fade ;
It passes with the hour :
 A faded rose can never be
 An emblem of my love for thee!"

"Then give me but thy word, —
A vow of love, — 't were better yet,"
 I cried ; "who once has heard
Such vows, can ne'er forget!
 If thou wilt give this pledge to me,
 Nor ring nor rose I 'll ask of thee!"

"O no!" she said again ;
"For spoken vows are empty breath,
 Whose memory is vain
When passion perisheth :

If e'er I lose my love for thee,
My vows must all forgotten be ! "

" Then what," I asked, " wilt thou,
O dearest ! to thy lover give ?
Nor ring nor rose nor vow
May I from thee receive ;
And yet some symbol should there be
To typify thy love for me ! "

Then dropped her silvery voice
Unto a whisper, soft and low :
" Here, take this gift, — my choice, —
The sweetest love can know ! "
She raised her head all lovingly,
And smiling, gave — a kiss to me !

MIGNON.

THINE is a little hand, —
  A tiny, little hand, —
  Yet if it clasp
  With timid grasp
My own, ah me! I well can understand
The pressure of that little hand!

  Thine is a little mouth, —
  A very little mouth, —
    Yet, ah! what bliss
    To steal a kiss,
Sweet as the honeyed zephyrs of the south,
From that same rosy little mouth!

  Thine is a little heart, —
  A little, fluttering heart, —

Yet is it warm
And pure and calm,
And loves me with its whole untutored art,
That fond and faithful little heart!

Thou art a little girl, —
Only a little girl, —
Yet art thou worth
The wealth of earth —
Diamond, and ruby, sapphire, gold, and pearl —
To me, thou blessèd little girl!

MINNIE'S ANSWER.

THERE 'S a certain girlish grace
  Hovers round thy form ;
Sits upon thy beaming face,
Sweetly blended with a trace
  Of a riper charm.
Should I say, " I love but thee,"
Minnie, were it safe for me ?

There 's a certain burning look
  Darting from thine eye, —
Reads my soul as 't were a book,
Searches every hidden nook
  E'en in passing by.
Shouldst thou fall in love with me,
Minnie, were it safe for thee ?

Then this loveliest of girls
  Raised her eyes to mine, —

          Minnie's Answer.

Smiled, and brushed away her curls,
Smiled, — with teeth like matchless pearls,
   Lips like matchless wine, —
And she softly said to me,
   " I would take my chance with thee."

AU COMBLE.

HEART of hearts and pearl of pearls,
    Dearest of all darling girls !
Can I make mere language say
How I love thee, night and day ?
Can I find, in head or heart,
Words to tell how fair thou art ?
Suns and moons may never shine
On a face and form like thine :
Rolling years may never see
Love more deep than mine for thee !
I have known diviner rest,
Softly pillowed on thy breast,
Than could ever haunt at night
Rosy couch of sybarite ;
And no music ever fell —
Song of bird, or silver bell —
Half so sweetly on my ear
As thy laughter, rich and clear !

Now, since love is life to us,
Let us love forever thus !
Knowing that a brighter day
Shall behold us joined for aye ;
For, to us, to love 't is given,
Here on earth and there in heaven.

SWEET IMPATIENCE.

I.

THE sunlight glimmers dull and gray
   Upon my wall to-day ;
  This summer is too long :
     The hot days go
     Weary and slow
As if time's reckoning were perverse and wrong :
     But when the flowers
Have faded, and their bloom has passed away,
     Then shall my song
     Be all of happier hours,
And more than one fond heart shall then be gay.

II.

But song can never tell
  How much I long to hear
One voice, that like the echo of a silver bell,

Unconscious, low, and clear,
Falls, as aforetime angel-voices fell
On Saint Cecelia's ear :
And it will come again,
And I shall hear it, when
The droning summer bee forgets his song
And frosty autumn crimsons hill and dell :
I shall not murmur, then,
" This summer is too long ! "

III.

The trellised grapes shall purple be,
And all
The forest aisles re-echo merrily
The brown quail's call,
And glossy chestnuts fall
In pattering plenty from the leafless tree
When autumn winds blow strong :
Then shall I see
Her worshipped face once more, and in its sun-
shine, I
Shall cease to sigh
" This summer is too long ! "

IV.

Meanwhile, I wander up and down
The noisy town,
Alone:
I miss the lithe form from my side,
The kind, caressing tone,
The gentle eyes
In whose soft depths so much of loving lies;
And lonely in the throng, —
Each jostling, bustling, grasping for his own, —
The weary words arise,
" This summer is too long!"

V.

Haste, happy hours, —
Fade, tardy, lingering flowers!
Your fragrance has departed, long ago;
I yearn .for cold winds, whistling through the
ruined bowers,
For winter's snow,
If with them, she
May come to teach my heart a cheerier song,

'And lovingly
Make me forget all weariness and severance and
        wrong,
  Whispering close and low,
  " Here are we still together, Love, although
The summer was so long ! "

AN AUTUMN JOY.

IT is a fair autumnal day,
  The ground is strewn with yellow leaves;
The maple stems gleam bare and gray,
  The grain is piled in golden sheaves;
Afar I hear the speckled quails
  Pipe shrill amid the stubble dry,
And muffled beats from busy flails
  Within the barn near by.

The latest roses now are dead,
  Their petals scattered far and wide,
The sumac-berries, richly red,
  Bedeck the lane on either side;
A dreamy calm is in the air,
  A dreamy echo on the sea:
Ah, never was a day more fair
  Than this, which comes to me!

I see the stacks of ripened corn,
The golden sunshine on the roof,
The diamond dew-drops of the morn,
That string with gems the spider's woof;
An azure haze is hanging low
About the outline of the hills,
And chanting sea-fowl southward go
From marshes, lakes, and kils.

For many years, the autumn brought
A plaintive sadness to my soul,
That shaded e'en my brightest thought,
And on my gayest moments stole;
'T was sad, yet sweet, a strange alloy
Of hope and sorrow intertwined:
This autumn brings me only joy,
No shadow haunts my mind.

And why is this? The dead leaves fall,
The blossoms wither, as of old,
And winter comes, with snowy pall,
To wrap the earth so deathly cold;

The sea-fowl, strung athwart the sky,
  Still chant their plaintive monotone ;
And why, when leaves and blossoms die,
  Should I feel joy alone ?

O, ask me not, — I dare not tell ;
  I must not all my heart disclose.
I think a fairy wove a spell
  About me, when decayed the rose !
Two gifts did dying summer bring, —
  Two symbols of undying bliss, —
Upon my finger glows a ring,
  Upon my lips, a kiss !

IN VAIN.

WHY were you kind, — O, why ?
  Why did you smile instead of frowning,
When Love in Lethe's wave was drowning ?
  Why were you kind, — O, why ?

  If you had looked on me
With scorn, or wrath, or cold disdaining,
My love for you had now been waning ;
  Why did you smile on me ?

  Long had I loved ; but Time,
Who softens all things, was beguiling
My weary heart, when, with your smiling,
  You came a second time !

  And now, alas ! again
I bear love's chains, and, musing lonely,

Hear your sweet voice and see you only, —
  Why were you kind again ?

    If all your love were dead,
Why did you kiss me, when we parted ?
Do we " forget," when broken-hearted ?
    Ah that I, too, were dead !

GONE.

THE summer was long and sweet,
  The roses blossomed for me
Over a porch where fairy feet
  Went pattering merrily.

All summer the roses smiled,
  Hiding their thorns from sight ;
All summer my passionate heart beat wild
  With a feverish love and delight.

Now, autumn's rain-drops beat
  On the casement, drearily ; —
The summer I found so long and sweet
  Has faded forever from me !

Under each thorny bough
  The roses are withering fast,
And my passionate heart beats slower, now,
  For the fever of love is past !

DE PROFUNDIS.

THROUGH the vague rifts in pearly clouds
that lie
Along the horizon, 'twixt sky and sea,
A planet's trembling radiance gleams on high,
Far, far from me.

The gentle breeze of evening loiters on,
Faint with the breath of many a tropic tree,
But groves of sandal, spice, and cinnamon
Are far from me.

O Love! I see thee glittering from afar;
Sweet airs and silvery lights encompass thee,
But — like the spice groves and the evening star —
Far, far from me!

A FAREWELL.

THE west-wind, laden with fragrance, blows,
  The dewdrops shine in the crimson rose ;
    — Is there something yet to tell ?
Ay, winds must pass and dewdrops fall ;
Naught that is gone can we recall :
    So now, dear Love, farewell !

Sweet lips prattle, and laugh, and sing,
White arms tenderly, closely cling ;
    — Is there something sad to tell ?
Ay, the sweet lips shall silent be,
And the arms unclasp in their agony :
    So now, dear Love, farewell !

Then is there nothing that God has made
That will not one day fall or fade ?
    — O Poet, in mercy tell !

Ay, love shall reign in these hearts of ours
When eyes, and lips, and wind-waved flowers
  Have known their last farewell.

For love is purer than dewdrops are,
The winds go never so wide and far,
  And none may truly tell
How, when the close caress is gone,
And words are silent, true love lives on,
  Never to say farewell !

VALE!

O GENTLEST season of the changing year,
  Though thy bright days are past,
Our hearts will ever hold thy memory dear
  So long as memories last:
Gladly each year we see thy pageant glow
Through amber days, with air like hydromel,
And now we sigh in whispers sad and slow,
  "Farewell, farewell!"

Through the dim vista of the forest nook
  Fall bars of shade and shine,
And o'er the shimmering ripples of the brook
  Swings the clematis vine:
The breeze comes faintly from the far-off sea
To linger in the leafy inland dell,
And sings October's dreamy monody,
  Farewell, farewell!

The withered meadow-grasses, white and brown,
  Gleam in the autumn air,
Where shining stars of silvery cotton-down
  Go sailing here and there :
Decadence sits upon the fading earth,
Her flowers have felt the touch of Azraël ;
To blooming sights and chirping sounds of mirth,
  Farewell, farewell !

The day declines, and cloudy phantoms drift
  About the distant west,
Where many a purple peak and golden rift
  Welcome the sun to rest :
As goes this happy day, the season goes,
Its dying murmurs chant the autumn's knell, —
The solemn requiem of the earth's repose, —
  Farewell, farewell !

Fade gently, gently, in the western sky,
  O fair October day !
Let rustling trees give back the parting sigh
  Of winds that die away !

Let the broad sunlight deepen into shade,
Let the kine homeward sound the tinkling bell,
To all thy glories that in twilight fade,
    Farewell, farewell !

The twittering birds may seek their hidden homes
    In the dark cedar-tree,
And hived bees, in honey-laden combs,
    Hum low and lazily :
O'er the wide landscape falls the shadowy night,
On field, and hill, and blue horizon's swell,
The sun gives forth his last expiring light, —
    Farewell, farewell !

EXPRESSION.

A HACKNEYED burden, to a hackneyed air,—
"I love thee only,—thou art wondrous fair!"
Alas! the poets have worn the theme threadbare!

Can I not find some words less tame and old,
To paint thy form and face of perfect mould,
Thy dewy lips, thy hair of brown and gold?

Can I not sing in somewhat fresher strain
The love I lavish and receive again,—
The thrilling joy, so like to thrilling pain?

Can I not, by some metaphor divine,
Describe the life I quaff like nectared wine
In being thine, and knowing thou art mine?

Ah, no ! this halting verse can naught express ;
No English words can half the truth confess,
That have not all been rhymed to weariness!

So let me cease my scribbling for to-day,
And maiden, turn thy lovely face this way, —
Words will not do, but haply kisses may !

THE TRYST.

O N speary grass and starry bloom
　　The tiny globes of dew are lying ;
The broad moon rises through the gloom
　　Of twilight haze ; and night-winds sighing
In long-drawn whispers say to me,
" 'T is eventide ... she comes to thee ! "

A heavy fragrance floods the air,
　　Where crimson roses climb and cluster ;
Heaven seems more near, and earth more fair,
　　The broad moon shines with holier lustre ;
A white robe through the dusk I see ...
O Joy ! O Love ! she comes to me !

PALINODE.

Athwart the west, where dies the day,
　　A stormy rack of cloud is drifting,

And round the uplands bleak and gray
  The wind its mournful voice is lifting :
With every moan it says to me ...
" 'T is night, but she comes not to thee ! "

Sharp thorns now grimly deck the bough
  Where clustered once the crimson roses :
With roses once she wreathed this brow
  Where now a thorny crown reposes.
A bitter past alone I see ...
Ah Heaven ! she comes no more to me !

AMONG THE HEATHER.

WINTRY winds are blowing cold
  On the moors of purple heather
Where, in sunnier days of old
Hand in hand we idly strolled,
  Thou and I together.
But those sunny days are past,
  And no more we walk together
Where the snow, on every blast,
  Whirls above the heather.

On the dreary moorland, now,
  In the storm I wander lonely,
Longing — love alone knows how —
For thy kiss on lip and brow,
  Longing for thee only :
Life can bring me naught but pain,
  Till among the purple heather
Hand in hand we walk again, —
  Thou and I together !

THE LEES OF LIFE.

I HAVE had my will,
　　Tasted every pleasure ;
I have drunk my fill
Of the purple measure ;
　It has lost its zest,
　Sorrow is my guest,
O, the lees are bitter, — bitter, —
　Give me rest !

　　Love once filled the bowl
Running o'er with blisses,
　Made my very soul
Drunk with crimson kisses ;
　But I drank it dry,
　Love has passed me by,
O, the lees are bitter, — bitter, —
　Let me die !

FARCEUR DE POETE!

SO, fare you well, true love, farewell !
    Did you think you saw an earnest woe
In the tear that just now flashed and fell ?
    It was not so ...
    I am a mere farceur, you know !

So, fare you well, true love ! you said,
    One fair June night, when the moon was low
That you would love me, living or dead ...
    I thought 't was so ...
    But I am a mere farceur, you know !

So, fare you well, true love ! though you
    Find peace and pleasure, here below,
I cannot : perhaps your heart is true ...
    I hope 't is so ...
    But I am a mere farceur, you know !

So, fare you well, true love ; we part !
　The paths diverge whereon we go :
'T is said I carry a broken heart ...
　Can that be so ? ...
　I am a mere farceur, you know !

Caricature of George Arnold
Henwitey.

BEER.

H ERE,
    With my beer
I sit,
While golden moments flit :
  Alas !
  They pass
Unheeded by :
And, as they fly,
I,
Being dry,
  Sit, idly sipping here
  My beer.

O, finer far
Than fame, or riches, are
The graceful smoke-wreaths of this free cigar !

Why
Should I
Weep, wail, or sigh?
What if luck has passed me by?
What if my hopes are dead, —
My pleasures fled?
Have I not still
My fill
Of right good cheer, —
Cigars and beer?

Go, whining youth,
Forsooth!
Go, weep and wail,
Sigh and grow pale,
Weave melancholy rhymes
On the old times,
Whose joys like shadowy ghosts appear, —
But leave to me my beer!
Gold is dross, —
Love is loss, —
So, if I gulp my sorrows down,

Or see them drown
In foamy draughts of old nut-brown,
Then do I wear the crown,
  Without the cross !

YOUTH AND AGE.

YOUTH hath many charms, —
    Hath many joys, and much delight ;
Even its doubts, and vague alarms,
    By contrast make it bright :
And yet — and yet — forsooth,
I love Age as well as Youth !

Well, since I love them both,
    The good of both I will combine, —
In women, I will look for Youth,
    And look for Age, in wine :
And then — and then — I 'll bless
This twain that give me happiness !

THE BUTTERFLY AND THE POET.

THE BUTTERFLY.

ON gorgeous wings he floateth along,
　　Little for this world careth he,
Save for the wild bee's somnolent song
　　And the sweets in flowers that be :
He sippeth to-day from the Lily's bell ;
To-morrow, he loveth the Rose as well.

THE POET.

ON gorgeous dreams he floateth along,
　　Nothing for this world careth he,
Save for the maidens' laughter and song
　　And the sweets on their lips that be :
To-day, blonde Edith he loveth well ;...
To-morrow, 't is brown-eyed Isabel.

CUI BONO?

A HARMLESS fellow, wasting useless days,
    Am I: I love my comfort and my leisure:
Let those who wish them, toil for gold and praise,
    To me, this summer-day brings more of pleasure.

So, here upon the grass I lie at ease,
    While solemn voices from the Past are calling,
Mingled with rustling whispers in the trees,
    And pleasant sounds of water idly falling.

There was a time when I had higher aims
    Than thus to lie among the flowers, and listen
To lisping birds, or watch the sunset's flames
    On the broad river's surface glow and glisten.

There was a time, perhaps, when I had thought
    To make a name, a home, a bright existence:

But time has shown me that my dreams were naught
   Save a mirage that vanished with the distance.

Well, it is gone : I care no longer now
   For fame, for fortune, or for empty praises ;
Rather than wear a crown upon my brow,
   I 'd lie forever here among the daisies.

So you, who wish for fame, good friend, pass by :
   With you I surely cannot think to quarrel :
Give me peace, rest, this bank whereon I lie,
   And spare me both the labor and the laurel !

THE GOLDEN FISH.

LOVE is a little golden fish,
    Wondrous shy ... ah, wondrous shy ...
You may catch him, if you wish,
He might make a dainty dish ...
    But I ...
    Ah, I 've other fish to fry !

For when I try to snare this prize,
    Earnestly, and patiently,
All my skill the rogue defies,
Lurking safe in Amy's eyes ...
    So you see,
    I am caught, and love goes free !

ÇA M'EST EGAL!

O, I WAS made for the present time!
    The present time was made for me!
I sing my song or weave my rhyme,
    From fear of future troubles free, —
    For they are naught to me!

'T is well with me at the present day:
    My brown-eyed Alice sits by me:
'T is true the moments pass away,
    And time is fleeting silently, —
    But that is naught to me!

I will not mourn for the silent past,
    Though pleasures fine it brought to me;
The present moments cannot last,
    But if they leave no vacancy,
    The past is naught to me!

I fill a bowl with rose-foamed wine,
My Alice quaffs a health to me ;
The present joyous day is mine,
The coming woe I cannot see, —
So that is naught to me !

And thus I find in the present time,
That life is fresh and sweet to me ;
I still will sit and weave my rhyme ;
The future soon will present be, —
And bring new joys to me !

GOLD AND PURPLE.

IN this little, old-fashioned garden of mine
   Poppies, and pinks, and pansies grow;
Yellow of gold and purple of wine
   Within their clustering blossoms glow;
And a purple ribbon is fluttering there,
From tangled ringlets of golden hair.

I love the pansies, poppies, and pinks,
   Their glistening eyes with the dewdrops wet:
I love them, — but in the garden, methinks,
   There is something that I love better yet;
For a purple ribbon is fluttering there,
From tangled tresses of golden hair.

PARTING.

WHITE and small was the hand I pressed
  Behind the rose-covered cottage door,
While the moon rode low in the azure west,
And the tremulous vines, by the wind caressed,
  Cast flickering shadows over the floor, —
Swinging, swaying, and sighing lowly,
"Perfect love is the one thing holy!"

Rosy and ripe were the lips I pressed
  Behind the rose-covered cottage door,
While the orioles slept in their downy nest
That swung in the vines, by the wind caressed,
  Casting weird shadows over the floor, —
But the wind in the tremulous vines sang ever,
"Love must perish and hearts must sever!"

THEN AND NOW.

YOU loved me once,... ah, well I knew it then !
　　One night you kissed me, underneath the
　　　　roses,
And said that we must never kiss again...
That was the parting... that strange moment,
　　　　when
　　The heart its weakness and its strength dis-
　　　　closes...
I knew you loved me then !

You love me yet... ah, well I know it now !
　　By these few stolen kisses, sad as tender,
That give my spirit strength, I know not how,
Falling like benisons on lip and brow
　　To fill my soul with mingled gloom and splen-
　　　　dor...
I know you love me now !

As then, and now, O let it be for aye !
　Let those dear lips still tell the sweet old story.
Let these kind kisses still drive grief away,
Lighten my heavy cross from day to day,
　And make my crown of thorns a crown of glory
For ever and for aye !

LOVE'S MESSENGERS.

I.

SUMMER winds, whispering over the rye,
Kissing the roses and hurrying by,
Where have ye latest been, O where?
Merrily tangling my maiden's hair, —
Wafting the tresses over her cheek, —
Playing among them at hide and seek,
Or trying with delicate scents of the south
To rival the breath from her own sweet mouth?
Tell me, summer winds, fresh and fair,
Where have ye latest been, O where?

But the balmy breezes floated away,
Daintily sighing, — no word said they.

II.

Bear ye no word from my maiden to me?
Did she not whisper her love to ye?

Ah, well do I know that her fondest dream
By the sun's warm light or the moon's pale beam
Is ever of me, and the love she bears
Oft breaks from her sweet lips, unawares.
Has she not murmured some tender word
That ye, as ye floated by, have heard?
Tell me, summer winds, frolic and free,
Bring ye no message from her to me?

But the balmy breezes frolicked away,
Daintily sighing, — no word said they.

III.

O faithless winds, since thus ye are still,
And bring no message my heart to thrill,
I will send ye again to my maiden's side
To tell her I 'll meet her at eventide;
Then fly, fly fast o'er the waving rye, —
The roses are lovely, but pass them by, —
Bid them to wait for the kisses they crave,
And linger not on the rivulet's wave:
Hasten, O summer winds, sighing above,
Tell her this night shall she meet her love!

The balmy breezes floated away,
And the roses wept that they would not stay.

IV.

Around the hill the summer winds sped,
Whirling and eddying overhead,
  Waving the moss on the cottage eaves,
  Rustling the feathery locust-leaves,
Brushing the dew-drops glimmering yet
On the odorous blooms of the mignonette,
  Till they reached a garden kept with care,
  And found a beautiful maiden there,
Alone in an arbor, where misty lines
Of sunshine fell through the tangled vines.

Then the balmy breezes sought her ear,
And the words they whispered were low but clear.

V.

They lifted the tresses of gold and brown
That over her snowy neck swept down,
  They said, in a musical, breezy voice,
  " Thy lover is coming, sweet child, rejoice !

When Hesperus' light in the west grows dim,
Thy lover will seek thee; be ready for him!"
  The maiden heard, and a rosy glow
  Flushed up to her cheek from her heart below,
And the summer winds caught, as they circled by,
Her perfumed breath in a gentle sigh.

Then the balmy breezes frolicked away,
And soon 'mong the rose-leaves nestled they.

LAZINESS.

MY window-curtain sweeps
    To and fro, in the lazy breeze,
As sea-weeds swing and sway in the deeps
    Of southern summer seas.

The lazy sunshine sleeps
    On the rose and snow of the apple-trees,
And lazy spring my spirit steeps
    In a lotos-dream of ease.

THE SIMPLE RHYME.

BENEATH the blue of summer skies,
　　Among the flowers of summer-time,
With loitering steps and half-closed eyes
　　I walk, and weave a simple rhyme.

The summer breezes go and come,
　　And blowing, musical and free,
Bring sounds of bees that idly hum
　　About the tangled briony.

Beneath the blue of summer skies,
　　Among the flowers of summer-time,
With loitering steps and dreamy eyes,
　　Fair maids shall sing my simple rhyme,

And may its echoes go and come
As fresh, as musical, as free,
As honey-bees that idly hum
About the tangled briony !

MEADOW–SWEET.

THE creamy banks of meadow-sweet
    Along the mill-stream's margin grow,
Where honey-bees with pollened feet
    Hum softly to and fro.

The sound is sweet, the fragrance rare,
    As summer breezes float along,
And round me all the summer air
    Is full of scent and song.

O, what to me are wealth and rank ?
    O, what are men, and their deceit ?
While I lie here, on the mill-stream's bank,
    Among the meadow-sweet !

FAREWELL TO SUMMER.

SUMMER is fading; the broad leaves that grew
　　So freshly green, when June was young, are
　　　　falling;
And, all the whisper-haunted forest through,
　　The restless birds in saddened tones are calling,
From rustling hazel copse and tangled dell,
　　"Farewell, sweet Summer,
　　　　Fragrant, fruity Summer,
　　　　　　Sweet, farewell!"

Upon the windy hills, in many a field,
　　The honey-bees hum slow, above the clover,
Gleaning the latest sweets its blooms may yield,
　　And, knowing that their harvest-time is over,
Sing, half a lullaby and half a knell,
　　"Farewell, sweet Summer,
　　　　Honey-laden Summer,
　　　　　　Sweet, farewell!"

The little brook that babbles 'mid the ferns,
   O'er twisted roots and sandy shallows playing,
Seems fain to linger in its eddied turns,
   And with a plaintive, purling voice, is saying,
(Sadder and sweeter than my song can tell,)
   " Farewell, sweet Summer,
      Warm and dreamy Summer,
        Sweet, farewell ! "

The fitful breeze sweeps down the winding lane
   With gold and crimson leaves before it flying ;
Its gusty laughter has no sound of pain,
   But in the lulls it sinks to gentle sighing,
And mourns the Summer's early broken spell, —
   " Farewell, sweet Summer,
      Rosy, blooming Summer,
        Sweet, farewell ! "

So bird, and bee, and brook, and breeze make
      moan,
   With melancholy song their loss complaining.
I too must join them, as I walk alone

Among the sights and sounds of Summer's wan-
ing ...
I too have loved the season passing well ...
So, farewell, Summer,
Fair but faded Summer,
Sweet, farewell!

SEPTEMBER.

S WEET is the voice that calls
    From babbling waterfalls
In meadows where the downy seeds are flying ;
    And soft the breezes blow,
    And eddying come and go,
In faded gardens where the rose is dying.

    Among the stubbled corn
    The blithe quail pipes at morn,
The merry partridge drums in hidden places,
    And glittering insects gleam
    Above the reedy stream
Where busy spiders spin their filmy laces.

    At eve, cool shadows fall
    Across the garden wall,
And on the clustered grapes to purple turning,

And pearly vapors lie
Along the eastern sky,
Where the broad harvest-moon is redly burning.

Ah, soon on field and hill
The winds shall whistle chill,
And patriarch swallows call their flocks together
To fly from frost and snow,
And seek for lands where blow
The fairer blossoms of a balmier weather.

The pollen-dusted bees
Search for the honey-lees
That linger in the last flowers of September,
While plaintive mourning doves
Coo sadly to their loves
Of the dead summer they so well remember.

The cricket chirps all day,
"O fairest Summer, stay!"
The squirrel eyes askance the chestnuts browning ;

The wild-fowl fly afar
Above the foamy bar
And hasten southward ere the skies are frowning.

Now comes a fragrant breeze
Through the dark cedar-trees
And round about my temples fondly lingers,
In gentle playfulness,
Like to the soft caress
Bestowed in happier days by loving fingers.

Yet, though a sense of grief
Comes with the falling leaf,
And memory makes the summer doubly pleasant,
In all my autumn dreams
A future summer gleams
Passing the fairest glories of the present !

THE HEART'S REST.

THE wind is idly blowing
　　And spilling its perfume rare;
The brook with its ceaseless flowing,
　　Is singing a quaint old air.

But night o'er nature comes stealing,
　　And the wind will die on the hill:
Cold winter's ice, congealing,
　　Will hush the song of the rill.

My heart, like the wind, is moaning,
　　The day seems heavy and long,
And memory's voice is droning
　　A sad, monotonous song.

But, heart, thou shalt rest at even,
	And memory's voice shall cease,
For the weary find rest in heaven,
	And the troubled shall be at peace.

THE SIREN OF THE ROSE.

ONCE in an ancient garden I found a maid,
Who sat, entranced by perfumes from many
a blossom ;
Between the trees the sunlight, down‑gliding,
played
Upon her shining tresses and snowy bosom :
She was so fair, I fancied she could but be
Some fairy thing, immortal, and more than
human ;
I gave her purest lilies : she answered me,
„ Die Rose ist die schönste von allen Blumen ! “

I offered her bright pansies, and meadow-sweet,
Great daffodils, and tulips in regal splendor,
I laid green wreaths of laurel before her feet,
And while I knelt her glances were dark and
tender :

Yet still she shook, though gently, her beauteous
    head ;
Who had resisted, surely, were one of few men !
And meekly still, in answer, she smiled and said,
    „ Die Rofe ift die fchönfte von allen Blumen ! "

I gazed about me, troubled : lo ! on my breast
    A crimson rose shone fairly, half bud, half
    blossom ;
I laid it, in its beauty, among the rest. . .
    She placed the fragrant secret within her bosom !
"Ah ! with it," cried I, stricken, "thou hast my
    heart !
I love thee, be thou fairy, or mortal woman !"
She whispered : "We are wedded, no more to part . . .
    Die Rofe ift die fchönfte von allen Blumen ! "

ON THE SANDS.

I MET Jessie Leigh
   On the sands;
Sweetly she smiled on me,
While breezes from the sea
   Brought dreamy odors as from distant lands,
And the warm sunshine fell
O'er weed, and pebble, and shell,
   Upon the sands.

I sat with Jessie Leigh
   On the sands;
Very fair was she,
And very kind to me;
   I kissed her forehead, and her dainty hands,
While the white moon above
Witnessed our vows of love,
   Upon the sands.

I saw Jessie Leigh
  On the sands ;
Cold and white lay she,
Drowned in the cruel sea,
  Her fair hair floating in dishevelled strands.
Would God I too had died,
And slept there by her side,
  Upon the sands !

FOUL WEATHER.

THE rain, upon the sodden grass,
　　Is beating, beating wearily ;
Gray clouds of mist, like phantoms, pass,
　　And the salt, wet wind wails drearily,
As it brings to me, from the shore afar,
The dirge of the surf on the outer bar.

My heart, within my fevered breast,
　　Is beating, beating wearily,
And memory, with a sad unrest,
　　Wails through its chambers drearily,
Till I almost wish that the surf afar
Were singing my dirge on the outer bar.

APART.

A WAVE, mid-ocean, sorrowed for the shore,
    "O, may I never see the smiling land?
Must I, then, break, and be a wave no more,
    Before I kiss the sand?"

A caged bird sang from early dawn till late,
    "Must I in gilded loneliness still pine,
Nor know the joy of nesting with my mate,
    Her rosy beak to mine?"

A tropic blossom drooped its bell above
    The northern loam: "O, may I never strew
My thirsty pollen in the blooms I love,
    And drink their honeyed dew?"

So I, O Love! am yearning for thy smile;
    So, mateless, I a sorrowing song upraise;

So for thy bloom I thirst and sigh, the while
  I count the weary days!

But though the wave may break its foamy crest,
  The bird be captive till its days are done,
The lonely blossom wither all unblest,
  Our lives shall yet be one!

AT DUSK.

A SHADOWY dance of ghostly images
By the red firelight on the wall is flung,
And ivory fingers on the ivory keys
Wake the old waltz we loved when love was
young.

On music is poetic fancy fed,
And these accords bring many a thought to
me,
Sad with the knell of hopes and pleasures dead,
Sweet with the promise of new joys to be.

In the warm firelight's glow thy shining hair
Seems half transmuted into precious gold,
And, faintly falling on the dusky air,
The olden cadence wakes the dream of old.

O Love ! the cup was bitter, but its lees
    Are sweet as honeyed dew in Hybla's flowers,
And all our days are fraught with prophecies
    Of sweeter draughts to come in future hours.

SERENADE.

I HEAR the dry-voiced insects call,
   And "Come," they say, "the night grows brief!"
I hear the dew-drops pattering fall
   From leaf to leaf, — from leaf to leaf.

Your night-lamp glimmers fitfully ;
   I watch below, you sleep above ;
Yet on your blind I seem to see
   Your shadow, love, — your shadow, love !

The roses in the night-wind sway,
   Their petals glistening with the dew ;
As they are longing for the day,
   I long for you, — I long for you

But you are in the land of dreams ;
   Your eyes are closed, your gentle breath

So faintly comes, your slumber seems
   Almost like death, — almost like death !

Sleep on ; but may my music twine
   Your sleep with strands of melody,
And lead you, gentle love of mine,
   To dream of me, — to dream of me !

VIA CRUCIS.

WHO treads the path of love and loss,
　　With humble steps and head bowed down,
May bear on earth the heaviest cross,
　　But wears in heaven the brightest crown.

Then let us bless the weary way,
　　The cross, the thorn, the cruel rod,
That lift us from our gods of clay
　　To know the true, the living God!

CHRISTMAS EVE.

O SUCH a wee, white stocking
    As Clare by the fireside hung,
When the Christmas-eve fire was waning
   And the Christmas-eve hymn was sung.
O, such a wee, wee stocking,
   So dainty, so snowily white,
That she hung on a branch of green holly,
   Ere bidding us all " Good-night ! "

What shall I put in her stocking ?
   Some pleasant book ? or a rhyme ?
Shall I write her a gentle lyric
   Of love and the holiday time ?
No : books are better for scholars ;
   At best they are silent friends ;
My rhymes, — alas ! they are many,
   But there their virtue ends.

Then what shall I put in the stocking
  That the hazel-eyed maiden hung
On a twig of red-berried holly
  When the Christmas-eve hymn was sung ?
Let me put my heart in the stocking
  — A fitting gift it would be ! —
But my heart is large, — it is boundless, —
  And the stocking is dainty and wee.

Well, here is the ring on my finger,
  I 've worn it many a year ;
'T was the gift of an ancient comrade
  Whose memory I hold dear.
Yet nothing on earth I treasure
  So much that she might not say, —
" O, give me this if you love me," —
  And bear it — a trophy — away !

So I drop my ring in the stocking
  — She knows it is mine full well.
(Good comrade, I prithee, forgive me !
  None other my love could tell.)

I drop my ring in the stocking
  So dainty, so snowy, so small, —
O Clare, as I cherish and love thee,
  May God love and cherish us all !

Ah me ! my heart is boundless,
  The stocking is dainty and wee ;
But love has a wonderful magic
  And wonderful power on me :
When I dropped my ring in the stocking,
  Breathing that earnest prayer,
My heart went in with the jewel,
  A present for maiden Clare.

NEW-YEAR'S EVE.

WITH a·bottle and a friend
　　—Friend is Tom and bottle sherry—
I shall now begin and end
This brief space where two years blend,
　　Wondrous wise and merry.

Never yet was there a woe
　　That had not a pleasure pressing
Close upon its heels ; and so
Through the Old and New we go,
　　Each at some time blessing.

Though the Old Year brought to me
　　Little joy and much of sorrow,
In the New I hope to be
Happier : my joys, you see,
　　Always come — to-morrow.

So, as New-Year's Eve doth end,
  Tom, and I, and golden sherry
— Finest wine and oldest friend —
Kill the space where two years blend,
  Making wondrous merry.

JUBILATE.

GRAY distance hid each shining sail,
    By ruthless breezes borne from me ;
And, lessening, fading, faint and pale,
    My ships went forth to sea.

Where misty breakers rose and fell
    I stood and sorrowed hopelessly ;
For every wave had tales to tell
    Of wrecks far out at sea.

To-day, a song is on my lips :
    Earth seems a paradise to me :
For God is good, and, lo, my ships
    Are coming home from sea !

STRAWBERRY FARMS, N. J.,
February, 1863.

THE MATRON YEAR.

I.

THE leaves that made our forest pathways
    shady
  Begin to rustle down upon the breeze;
The year is fading, like a stately lady
  Who lays aside her youthful vanities:
Yet, while the memory of her beauty lingers,
  She cannot wear the livery of the old,
So Autumn comes, to paint with frosty fingers
  Some leaves with hues of crimson and of gold.

II.

The Matron's voice filled all the hills and valleys
  With full-toned music, when the leaves were
    young;
While now, in forest dells and garden-alleys,
  A chirping, reedy song at eve is sung;

Yet sometimes, too, when sunlight gilds the morn-
    ing,
  A carol bursts from some half-naked tree,
As if, her slow but sure decadence scorning,
  She woke again the olden melody.

III.

With odorous May-buds, sweet as youthful pleasures,
  She made her beauty bright and debonair :
But now, the sad earth yields no floral treasures,
  And twines no roses for the Matron's hair :
Still can she not all lovely things surrender ;
  Right regal is her drapery even now, —
Gold, purple, green, inwrought with every splendor,
  And clustering grapes in garlands on her brow !

IV.

In June, she brought us tufts of fragrant clover
  Rife with the wild bee's cheery monotone,
And, when the earliest bloom was past and over,
  Offered us sweeter scents from fields new-mown :

Now, upland orchards yield, with pattering
    laughter,
  Their red-cheeked bounty to the groaning wain,
And heavy-laden racks go creeping after,
  Piled high with sheaves of golden-bearded grain.

v.

Erelong, when all to love and life are clinging,
  And festal holly shines on every wall,
Her knell shall be the New-Year bells, outringing ;
  The drifted snow, her stainless burial-pall :
She fades and fails, but proudly and sedately,
  This Matron Year, who has such largess given,
Her brow still tranquil, and her presence stately,
  As one who, losing earth, holds fast to heaven !

REQUIESCAM.

G IVE me, when I die,
    A grave among the corn and clover.
Let me peaceful lie
In some field, with forests nigh,
Where the blossoms bending over
    Mingle sigh for sigh
With ever rustling leaves
Whispering to the rustling sheaves.

    Let the tall grass wave
    High above my grave,
And strew, each fall, their treasures o'er me ;
    Leaves of gold, and brown,
    Softly floating down,
Or driven wildly onward, when 't is stormy.

    O give me not a tomb
White, and marble-cold, and dreary,

In the churchyard's gloom !
Rather, when I 'm weary,
Let me lie at rest
    'Neath the clover, growing fair,
    In the warm, sunshiny air,
With its thready tendrils twining round my
      breast.

    So, tranquil be my sleep,
When the hazy, slanting beams
    Rest on forest, vale, and steep,
Through long, summer afternoons
    Be my slumber still and deep.
Let the new and waning moons
Come, and go, and bring me dreams.

IN THE DARK.

[While this book was passing through the press, a fortunate accident placed in my possession the original manuscript of this, the last poem that Arnold wrote. It was written within a few days of his death, when the shadow of the night that knows no earthly dawn was already closing around him. — W. W.]

ALL moveless stand the ancient cedar-trees
    Along the drifted sand-hills where they
       grow ;
And from the dark west comes a wandering
      breeze,
    And waves them to and fro.

A murky darkness lies along the sand,
    Where bright the sunbeams of the morning
      shone ;
And the eye vainly seeks, by sea and land,
    Some light to rest upon.

No large, pale star its glimmering vigil keeps ;
  An inky sea reflects an inky sky ;
And the dark river, like a serpent, creeps
  To where its black piers lie.

Strange, salty odors through the darkness steal,
  And through the dark the ocean-thunders roll :
Thick darkness gathers, stifling, till I feel
  Its weight upon my soul !

I stretch my hands out in the empty air ;
  I strain my eyes into the heavy night ;
Blackness of darkness !... Father, hear my prayer...
  Grant me to see the light !

POEMS GRAVE AND GAY.

(1867.)

I.

GRAVE.

"'T is also well this air is stirred
   By nature's voices loud and low, —
The thunder and the chirping bird,
   And grasses whispering as they grow."

R. M. Milnes [Lord Houghton].

A SUMMER LONGING.

I MUST away to wooded hills and vales,
  Where broad, slow streams flow cool and
    silently,
And idle barges flap their listless sails. . . .
For me the summer sunset glows and pales,
  And green fields wait for me.

I long for shadowy forests, where the birds
  Twitter and chirp at noon from every tree.
I long for blossomed leaves and lowing herds:
And nature's voices say, in mystic words,
  'The green fields wait for thee.'

I dream of uplands, where the primrose shines,
  And waves her yellow lamps above the lea;
Of tangled copses, swung with trailing vines;
Of open vistas, skirted with tall pines,
  Where green fields wait for me.

I think of long, sweet afternoons, when I
    May lie and listen to the distant sea,
Or hear the breezes in the reeds that sigh,
Or insect-voices chirping shrill and dry,
    In fields that wait for me.

These dreams of summer come to bid me find
    The forest's shade, the wild bird's melody,
While summer's rosy wreaths for me are twined,
While summer's fragrance lingers on the wind,
    And green fields wait for me.

FIRE-FLIES.

'TIS June, and all the lowland swamps
   Are rich with tufted reeds and ferns,
And filmy with the vaporous damps
   That rise when twilight's crimson burns;
And as the deepening dusk of night
Steals purpling up from vale to height,
The wanton fire-flies show their fitful light.

Soft gleams on clover-beams they fling,
   And glimmer in each shadowy dell,
Or downward with a sudden swing
   Fall, as of old a Pleiad fell;
And on the fields bright gems they strew
And up and down the meadow go,
And through the forest wander to and fro.

They store no hive nor earthy cell,
   They sip no honey from the rose;

By day unseen, unknown they dwell,
　Nor aught of their rare gift disclose;
Yet, when the night upon the swamps,
Calls out the murk and misty damps,
They pierce the shadows with their shining lamps.

Now ye, who in life's garish light,
　Unseen, unknown, walk to and fro,
When death shall bring a dreamless night,
　May ye not find your lamps aglow?
God works, we know not why nor how,
And, one day, lights, close hidden now,
May blaze like gems upon an angel's brow.

A SUNSET FANTASIE.

WHEN the sun sets over the bay,
    And sweeping shadows solemnly lie
On its mottled surface of azure and gray,
    And the night-winds sigh, —
Come, O Leonore, brown-eyed one,
To the cloudy realms of the setting sun!
    Where crimson crag, and silvery steep,
    And amaranth rift, and purple deep,
Look dimly soft, as the sunset pales,
Like the shadowy cities of ancient tales.

As Egypt's queen went floating along
    To her lover, when all the orient air
Was laden with echoes of dreamy song,
    And the plash of oars, and perfumes rare,
        So will we float,
        In a golden boat,

On velvet cushions soft and wide;
I and my love, the onyx-eyed,
Will watch the twilight radiance fail, —
   Cheek by cheek and side by side, —
And. our mingled breath, O Leonore,
Shall fan the silken sail,
   To the shining line of that fairy strand
   Where sky is water and cloud is land, —
The wonderful sunset shore!

On those dim headlands, here and there,
   The lofty glacier-peaks between,
Through the purple haze of the twilight air,
   The tremulous glow of a star is seen.
There let us dwell, O Leonore,
   Free from the griefs that haunt us here,
   Knowing nor frown, nor sigh, nor tear:
There let us bide forevermore,
   Happy for aye in the sunset sphere!

In the mountainous cloudland, far away,
Behold, a glittering chasm gleams!

O, let us cross the heaving bay,
To that land of love and dreams!
  There would I lie, in a misty bower,
Tasting the nectar of thy lip,
Sweet as the honeyed dews that drip
  From the budding lotos-flower!
Dip the oar and spread the sail
For shining peak and shadowy vale!
  Fill, O sail, and plash, O oar,
  For the wonderful sunset shore!

ART AND NATURE.

I.

IN the dusk of summer even, when the roses
    slowly swayed
To and fro, in gentle breezes that around the
    trellis played,
And the rising moon wrought wonders of fan-
    tastic light and shade,
I walked up and down with Florence, under-
    neath the linden-trees,
Listening to the ocean murmurs, rising, falling,
    with the breeze . . .
Murmurs faint but fraught with music, hints of
    dreams and prophecies.

II.

Far below us, where the beetling cliff its dizzy
    depth sheered down,

We could hear the song and laughter of the
    merry-making town, —
That the murmurs of the ocean and the wind
    were vain to drown ;
And above the rocks there flaunted, now and
    then, a lurid light,
As the harshly hissing rocket climbed along its
    fiery height,
Piercing, with its savage splendor, the soft
    beauty of the night.

III.

Noise of drums and trumpets mingled with the
    cadence of the seas ;
Bursts of wine-begotten laughter soiled the fresh-
    ness of the breeze ;
And the heavy tramp of soldiers shook the lofty
    linden-trees.
There, upon a rustic sofa, where the moonlight
    ··whitely slept,
And a rustic roof gave shelter from the dew
    that heaven wept,

We sat down to break the silence that till then
    we both had kept.

IV.

Florence said: "How grates this feasting, this
    wild noise of blatant mirth,
On the holy peace that hovers o'er the ocean
    and the earth!
Why should man's best sense of pleasure to
    such sights and sounds give birth?
Why not seek a calm expression for fulfilment
    of desire?
Must our triumphs and successes all be writ in
    words of fire, —
Words that leave but bitter ashes when their
    fitful sparks expire?

V.

"Thus it is with men ... they trample on the
    dignity of man ...
With our purest joys have mingled, ever since
    the world began,

Brazen blasts, and blazing rockets, and the deaf-
    ening rataplan!
Yet the moon in silent grandeur rises from the
    flashing sea,
And the stars burn on forever, and the winds
    blow ever free,
Calm, yet joyous, with an inner sense of holy
    ecstasy."

VI.

"Yes," I said, "'t is in our nature; we are
    somehow coarsely made;
And we think that our emotions, to be real,
    must be displayed;
That our feelings must be measured by our
    folly and parade.
Yet, perhaps, we err not greatly; man needs
    symbols, and we find
In this fire and smoke and clamor that seethe
    upward on the wind
Some external type of triumph gained by sword
    or gained by mind.

VII.

" Thus, the deepest-thinking student, when his
    daily task is done
And his cloister is illumined by the last rays
    of the sun,
Lays his ponderous ancient volumes in their
    alcove, one by one,
And goes forth to seek companions in the cellar
    or the hall,
Where the clinking of the goblets, and the dan-
    cing-leader's call,
And the hum of pleasant music on his weary
    ear may fall."

VIII.

Florence took the word up quickly : "Ay, your
    parallel is true ;
And that all you men thus trifle is the greater
    shame for you !
Are no deities more worthy than the mad Bac-
    chante crew ?

O you men! the wise and simple to the self-
    same tenets cling;
To the search for sensuous pleasures you your
    highest talents bring,
And your peals of shallow laughter through the
    holiest chambers ring!

IX.

You . . . confess it, now! . . are longing to be
    yonder, down below,
Where through thick, black clouds of smoke de-
    moniac bonfires redly glow,
Like the old, fiend-lighted beacons on the Brocken
    long ago!
You too love the brazen clamor, rattling drum,
    and trumpet's strain,
And the gaudy rocket cutting this fair, moonlit
    sky in twain,
More than grand old ocean's music and the
    calm of Hesper's reign!"

X.

"No," I said, "you judge us harshly; wine and
    laughter are not ends,
They are means to that enjoyment whereto
    every spirit tends;
And 't is wise that man his labor with his pleas-
    ure sometimes blends.
Would you have us all ascetics, scorning what
    our natures crave,
Toiling on, and noting nothing of the outer
    fabric, save
It might be a gilded sunset, or the moonlight
    on the wave?"

XI.

As I spoke, a filmy vapor, edged with pearl and
    silver gray,
Passed across the moon's broad circle, as it
    floated on its way,
And a glittering path of diamonds far athwart
    the ocean lay:

All the heavenly vault seemed opened where
    the moon in ether rode,
And like Cleopatra's jewels on the dusk the
    planets glowed,
While, below, the smoky bonfires made a vulgar
    palinode.

XII.

"There!" said Florence, then outstretching her
    white hand toward the sea,
"Dian thus asserts her greatness, — her fair right
    of royalty;
Keep you all your baleful beacons, — leave the
    moon and stars to me!"
Then she drew her robe about her, for the air
    was growing chill,
And we homeward strolled together, by the path
    around the hill,
Silently, and gazing seaward, where the moon-
    path glittered still.

PSYCHE.

HER feet, they are so small,
 So delicate her tread,
The daisies do not bend at all
 When she walks overhead ;
But each looks up, and falls in love
With Psyche's tiny feet above.

She walks with such an art,
 And steps so daintily,
If she should tread upon my heart,
 'T would still unbroken be ;
Unless 't were by the loveliness
Which Psyche's tiny feet possess !

MY WIND-HARP.

WHAT faint, sad sounds are these, the air
    pervading?
Rising and falling with the winds that blow;
Now keenly clear, like elfish serenading,
    And now like angel-music, sweet and low.

Is it the gentle breeze of summer, mourning
    Over its loved June roses' early death?
Or doth Azraël give a solemn warning
    To those he claims, with such melodious breath?

No: 't is my wind-harp, in the window lying ...
    I love to hear it, while I string sad rhymes;
For its faint tones, like ghosts of dead songs, sigh-
      ing,
    Bring me quaint fancies of the olden times.

SEA-SHORE FANCIES.

O PLEASANT waters, rippling on the sand,
   Green and pellucid as the beryl-stone,
With crested breakers heaving toward the land,
   Chanting their ceaseless breezy monotone,
What snowy little feet at girlish play
Have ye not kissed on Newport's beach to-day?

O waves, that foam around yon lonely rock,
   Boding the distant storm with hoarser roar,
Has not some ship, beneath the tempest's shock,
   Gone down, a piteous wreck, to rise no more?
Lost in the mighty billows' wash and sway,
What gallant hearts have ye not stilled to-day?

O dancing breakers, fresh from other seas
   Whereon the lingering, loving sunshine smiles,
Your spray is fragrance, on the fragrant breeze,

Borne from the spice-groves of those palmy isles
Where dusky maids make merriment alway, —
Have ye not laved their perfect forms to-day?

O tossing billows, come ye from afar
  Where over ice-fields the aurora beams,
Dimming the radiance of the northern star
    That through the lengthened night of winter
      gleams
Upon the toppling icebergs, grim and gray, —
Have ye not lashed their frozen sides to-day?

O sea of life, whose waters heave and roll,
  Ye lave sad wrecks and joyous youthful forms:
Ye bring sweet fragrance to the weary soul,
  And chill it with the breath of icy storms:
Here on the shore we smile and weep and pray, —
O waves, cleanse all our sins from us to-day!

THE OMEN.

A STORM is gathering in the seaward sky,
The sunlit islands in its shadow die,
And startled sea-gulls on the wind flap by.

Yet, faint and far, a single sunset ray
Slants o'er the waters many a mile away,
Making yon sail a Pleiad gone astray.

That ray is like one hope that lingers still
Through fears that sicken and through doubts
that chill —
The victory of passion over will!

The black clouds thicken: well, so let it be:
But while yon sunlit sail I still can see,
I will believe that there is hope for me!

The shadows spread along the horizon,
... It faints ... it fades ; the sail is almost gone,
And with it pales the hope just now that shone.

'T is gone ! The waves upon the rocky shore
Break heavily, with hoarse and hungry roar,
And hope has vanished, to return no more !

SEPTEMBER DAYS.

IN flickering light and shade the broad stream
    goes,
  With cool, dark nooks and checkered, rippling
    shallows ;
Through reedy fens its sluggish current flows,
  Where lilies grow and purple-blossomed mallows.

The aster-blooms above its eddies shine,
  With pollened bees about them humming slowly,
And in the meadow-lands the drowsy kine
  Make music with their sweet bells, tinkling
    lowly.

The shrill cicala, on the hillside tree,
  Sounds to its mate a note of love or warning ;
And turtle-doves re-echo, plaintively,
  From upland fields, a soft, melodious mourning.

A golden haze conceals the horizon,
    A golden sunshine slants across the meadows;
The pride and prime of summer-time is gone,
    But beauty lingers in these autumn shadows.

The wild-hawk's shadow fleets across the grass,
    Its softened gray the softened green outvying;
And fair scenes fairer grow while yet they pass,
    As breezes freshen when the day is dying.

O sweet September! thy first breezes bring
    The dry leaf's rustle and the squirrel's laughter,
The cool, fresh air, whence health and vigor spring,
    And promise of exceeding joy hereafter.

GOLDEN-ROD.

LIKE the nodding crest of a golden helm,
  When the autumn west-wind bloweth,
Among the thickets of birch and elm
  On the steep hillside it groweth.
There, when summer was young and fair,
And wild-wood roses scented the air,
I sat with hazel-eyed maiden Clare....
      Alack! who knoweth
      How love goeth?
The hazel-eyed one was fickle as gay;
.The wild-wood roses have faded away;
And the golden-rod blooms on their graves to-day!

Well, let a golden peace uprise
  On the grave where my passion lieth!
Let me forget the hazel eyes!
  As the bee, that southward hieth,

Forgetteth the wild-wood roses fair
When the golden-rod shineth upon the air,
So let me forget the maiden Clare !
> Alack ! who knoweth
> How love goeth ?
Why should I sigh for Clare alway ?
Genevieve's eyes have a gentler sway ;
And she smiled — ah, sweetly ! — on me to-day !

OCTOBER.

O'ER hill and field October's glories fade;
   O'er hill and field the blackbirds southward
      fly;
The brown leaves rustle down the forest glade,
Where naked branches make a fitful shade,
   And the last blooms of autumn withered lie.

The berries on the hedgerow ripen well,
   Holly and cedar, burning bush and brier;
The partridge drums in some half-hidden dell,
Where all the ground is gemmed with leaves that
      fell,
   Last storm, from the tall maple's crown of fire.

The chirp of crickets and the hum of bees
   Come faintly up from marsh and meadow land,
Where reeds and rushes whisper in the breeze,

And sunbeams slant between the moss-grown
    trees,
  Green on the grass and golden on the sand.

From many a tree whose tangled boughs are bare
  Lean the rich clusters of the clambering vine ;
October's mellow hazes dim the air
Upon the uplands, and the valley where
  The distant steeples of the village shine.

Adown the brook the dead leaves whirling go ;
  Above the brook the scarlet sumacs burn ;
The lonely heron sounds his note of woe
In gloomy forest-swamps where rankly grow
  The crimson cardinal and feathery fern.

Autumn is sad : a cold, blue horizon
  Darkly encircles checkered fields and farms,
Where late the gold of ripening harvests shone :
But bearded grain and fragrant hay are gone,
  And autumn moans the loss of summer's
    charms.

Yet, though our summers change and pass away,
  Though dies the beauty of the hill and plain,
Though warmth and color fade with every day,
Our hearts shall change not, for hope seems to say
  That all our dearest joys shall come again.

And if the flowers we nurture with such care
  Must wither, though bedewed with many tears,
They shall arise in some diviner air,
To bloom again, more fragrant and more fair,
  And gladden us through all the coming years.

The sun sinks slowly toward the far-off west;
  The breeze is freshening from the far-off shore;
So come, fair eve, and bring to every breast
That sense of tranquil joy, of gentle rest,
  We knew in happy autumns gone before!

SUMMER AND AUTUMN.

GORGEOUS leaves are whirling down,
　　Homeward comes the scented hay,
O'er the stubble, sear and brown,
　　Flaunt the autumn flowers gay:
　　　　Ah, alas!
　　　　Summers pass, —
Like our joys, they pass away!

Fanned by many a balmy breeze,
　　In the spring I loved to lie
'Neath the newly budded trees,
　　Gazing upward to the sky:
　　　　But, alas!
　　　　Time will pass,
And the flowers of spring must die!

Oft my maiden sat with me,
  Listening to the thrush's tone,
Warbled forth from every tree
  Ere the meadow hay was mown:
      But, alas!
      Summers pass, —
Now, I wander all alone!

Love, like summer-time, is fair,
  Decked with buds and blossoms gay;
But upon this autumn air
  Floats a voice, which seems to say
      "Loves, alas!
      Also pass,
As the summers pass away!"

THE MERRY CHRISTMAS TIME.

GREEN were the meadows with last summer's
       store ;
The maples rustled with a wealth of leaves ;
The brook went babbling to the pebbly shore,
Down by the old mill, with its cobwebbed door,
      And swallow-haunted eaves ;
And all the air was warm, and calm, and clear,
As if cold winter never could come near.

Now, the wide meadow-lands where then we
      strolled
  Are misty with a waste of whirling snow :
The ruined maples, stripped of autumn's gold,
Sigh mournfully and shiver in the cold,
      As the hoarse north-winds blow.
Yet something makes this frosty season dear,...
The Merry, Merry Christmas time is here.

The Merry Christmas, with its generous boards,
  Its fire-lit hearths, and gifts, and blazing trees,
Its pleasant voices uttering gentle words,
Its genial mirth, attuned to sweet accords,
        Its holy memories!
The fairest season of the passing year,...
The Merry, Merry Christmas time is here.

The sumacs by the brook have lost their red;
  The mill-wheel in the ice stands dumb and still;
The leaves have fallen and the birds have fled;
The flowers we loved in summer all are dead,
        And wintry winds blow chill.
Yet something makes this dreariness less drear,...
The Merry, Merry Christmas time is here.

Since last the panes were hoar with Christmas
        frost
  Unto our lives some changes have been given; —
Some of our barks have labored, tempest-tossed,
Some of us, too, have loved, and some have lost,
        Some found their rest in heaven.

So, humanly, we mingle smile and tear,
When Merry Christmas time is drawing near.

Then pile the fagots higher on the hearth,
  And fill the cup of joy, though eyes be dim.
We hail the day that gave our Saviour birth,
And pray His spirit may descend on earth,
    That we may follow Him.
'T is this that makes the Christmas time so dear :
Christ, in His love for us, seems drawing near.

THE POET'S AWAKENING.

LONG had he been a thing of common clay,
    A being of earthly mould ;
But, lo ! an angel crossed his path, one day,
    And turned the clay to gold.

Silent was he : the angel came again,
    And, as she passed along,
She kissed his lips all lovingly, and then
    He opened them in song.

JACOB'S LADDER.

IT was a prophet slept;
   And in his dream vast mysteries were
        seen, —
  A vapory cloud, that seemed to lower and lift,
  Pierced in its centre by a glittering rift,
With splendid glimpses of the heaven between; —
    And still the prophet slept.

    A ladder from the earth
Far-slanting touched the opening of the cloud.
  Thereon the prophet saw fair figures go,
  With stately steps, serenely to and fro, —
Fair angels, filmy-winged and tranquil-browed,
    Between the heaven and earth.

    O prophet's dream of heaven!
Do I unfold your mystery aright?

Was not that ladder typical of love,
That leads us to our glorious home above,
And, thronged with angels, tranquil-browed and
bright,
Makes earth seem near to heaven?

HER EYES.

THOSE eyes!... those eyes!...
　　O maiden, turn those eyes away!
My best ambition faints and dies
　　Beneath their gentle sway.
I list not fame's loud trumpet-call,
　　But idly sit and linger still,
A slave within the pleasant thrall
　　Of those deep eyes and thy sweet will.

Those eyes!... those eyes!...
　　While haunted by their lustrous gleam,
I care not to be great or wise,
　　And life seems like a dream.
The golden hours unnoted fly,
　　From idle night to idle day:
My books and pen neglected lie —
　　O maiden, turn those eyes away!

ENOUGH.

NOTHING for sordid, golden dross I care,
    Little of worldly wealth care I to hold!
Seek her I love: look on her shining hair,—
    Is it not wealth of gold?

I am not envious of the diamond's flash;
    Its wondrous brilliance dazzleth not my sight;
For her sweet eyes, beneath their fringed lash,
    Make dim the diamond's light.

I care no more for music's dreamy swell;
    Nor flute nor viol greatly pleaseth me;
Her speech is softer than a silver bell,
    Her laugh is melody.

I leave the wine which once I loved to sip:
    Why should I drain the crimson beaker dry,
When there is subtle nectar on her lip
    That I may drink—and die?

MIDNIGHT MUSIC.

WHEN the sun has passed away,
   When the night has crowned the day,
And the planet's trembling radiance
Rules above with gentle sway;

Through the sighing poplar-trees
Floats a cadence on the breeze, —
Up into the moonlit heaven,
Out across the moonlit seas.

In the grand old garden, near,
Manly voices, singing clear,
Mingled with the quivering viol,
Pierce the midnight atmosphere.

O, 't is sweet, when day has flown,
By the casement, all alone,

Thus to sit, and drink, like nectar,
Midnight music's regal tone!

Lady, whosoe'er thou art,
Seest thou him who stands apart?
None could sing thus save a lover,
And his song should win thy heart!

WINE SONG.

A S I pour the wine,
I behold its sparkles bright : —
    'T is the light
Beaming, lady mine,
In those eyes of thine, —
    Beaming deeply bright.

    As I pour the wine,
I behold its rosy flush : —
    'T is the blush
Mantling, lady mine,
That fair face of thine, —
    Rosy-tinted blush.

    As I pour the wine,
Its fragrance I descry : —
    'T is the sigh

Coming, lady mine,
From that mouth of thine, —
  Love's half-stifled sigh.

  As I drink the wine,
Thrills my heart with sudden bliss : —
  Like the kiss
That proclaims thee mine. . . .
Is there aught divine
  Save a lover's kiss ?

SERENADE.

I.

IN deepest sleep my lady lies ;
   Fairer than ever now she seems ;
Her drooping lashes veil her eyes,
   That see, mayhap, her love in dreams ;
And her soft breath, that comes and goes,
   Is balmy with a scent more rare
And fragrant than the loveliest rose
   Whose odor lingers on the air !

II.

In deepest sleep my lady lies,
   Nor hears her lover singing here ;
The night-wind murmurs lullabies,
   That soothe and charm her slumbering ear ;
Athwart the trees the moonbeams fall ;
   Along the sky a meteor gleams ;

The whip-poor-wills unceasing call, —
    Yet still she sleeps, and, sleeping, dreams !

III.

In deepest sleep my lady lies ;
    The moonlit moments are not long,
While here, beneath the summer skies,
    I open all my heart in song.
Upon her couch the moonlight sleeps,
    The envious roses drop a tear, —
The proudest of them, even, weeps
    To think she may not nestle near.

THE OLD RAMBLE.

THE cedar hedge is darkly green,
   Its shade lies cool upon the clover,
And branches make a goodly screen
With glimpses dimly caught between
   Of blue skies arching over.

About the cedars thickly twine
   The tendrilled woodbine's mazy tangles,
And the wild blackberry's graceful vine
With white, bee-haunted blooms that shine
   Like sunlit silver spangles.

There, when the summer south wind sighs,
   I sit with swaying boughs above me,
And gaze into the cloudless skies,
As deeply azure as the eyes
   Of her who used to love me.

The suns and moons of many a year
　　Have waxed and waned and faded slowly
Since we together rambled here ;
Yet every path we trod is dear,
　　Each spot she loved is holy !

This gray old stone, on which we sat
　　So oft to rest us in our rambles,
Seems still an ancient friend, but that
Its lichened surface broad and flat
　　Is overgrown with brambles.

I sit me down beneath the trees,
　　Where, green and gold, the sunshine dances,
And dreamy sounds of droning bees,
And distant bells, upon the breeze,
　　Awaken olden fancies.

O, bees that in the sunshine sing,
　　And round the starry blossoms hover,
What sweet, sad thoughts your dronings bring
Of days when life was in its spring,
　　And I a happy lover !

O, distant bells, that swinging slow,
　Recall the pleasant days departed,
Your silvery voices, soft and low,
Rang in her wedding, long ago,
　And left me broken-hearted !

ALONE BY THE SHORE.

I WALK by the shore, by the shore, —
  I walk by the shore of the sounding sea,
And hear in its endless, thunderous roar
  A summoning voice to me.

I sit on the sand, on the sand,
  The foam and the froth go swirling by;
The wind whispers gently over the land,
  And seems like a human sigh; —

A sigh for a friend, for a friend, —
  A calm and a true and a noble soul,
Whose friendship and faith might nevermore end,
  As long as these breakers roll.

Far out in the west, in the west,
  The sun through his robe of vapor gleams;

And so, like a king, right royally dressed,
  Goes down to the land of dreams.

I look on my life, on my life,
  A selfish battle it seems to me ;
I long for rest from its terrible strife,
  Far down in the deep, deep sea.

I walk by the shore, by the shore,
  And still as I gaze on the fading west,
I list to the voice with its thunderous roar, —
  "O come, for the dead find rest!"

I WANT NOT LOVE.

I WANT not love, but who will be my friend ?
   I feel the need of some kind soul, to strew
   My way with blossoms, as I wander slow
Down toward the valley where all paths must end....
Can I not find a friend ?

I want not love, — I only want a friend.
   Love's joys are rapture, but its pains are death ;
   And joys and pains to love are food and
      breath ;
So, when these weary arms I would extend,
Let them enfold a friend !

I want not love, — ah no ! I want a friend !
   Why should a broken heart be tortured still ?
   Have I not had of misery my fill ? ...
But thou who readest what I here have penned, —
Wilt thou not be my friend ?

IN THE ORGAN-LOFT.

THE dead in their ancient graves are still;
  There they 've slept for many a year ;
The last faint sunbeams glance o'er the hill,
  Gilding the dry grass, tall and sear,
And the foam of the babbling rill.

Into the church the ruddy light falls,
  Through rich stained windows, narrow and high ;
Pictures. it paints on the old, gray walls,
  Scenes from the days that have long gone by, —
And hark ! — 't is my Rosalie calls !

She calls my name, — I have heard it oft
  Just at the golden sun's decline :
I answer the call, so sweet and soft ;
  And, turning, see where her bright eyes shine,
High up in the organ-loft.

I pass the winding and narrow stair ;
　The gallery door stands open wide ;
I know no shadow of pain nor care,
　While darling Rosalie stands by my side,
In the sunset light so fair.

What grand old hymns and chants we sang, —
　Grand old chants that I loved so well ;
And the organ's tones, — how they pealed and rang,
　Piercing the heart, no tongue can tell,
With what a delicious pang !

O those hours ! what holy light
　Hovers around when their memories rise !
Music, love, and the sunset bright,
　Tenderest glances from Rosalie's eyes,
And a long, sweet kiss, for good-night !

THE BROKEN CAVALIER'S SONG.

["'Well,' said Don Sebastian, 'our Spanish wine is sweet, if life is bitter!'
And, taking up the mandoline, with a kind of sad gayety, he began to sing." —
Don Sebastian de Cerveñas.]

THE jolly old world goes rolling round, —
  Drink wine, brothers mine!
The dead lie sleeping under ground, —
  Drink wine! 't is this we're drinking
Kills all care and stops all thinking.
  Drink wine, beverage fine!
See through the goblets the rosy light shine:
Happiness lies in a flagon of wine!

The maiden I loved was fair to see, —
  Drink wine, brothers mine!
But long ago she jilted me, —
  Drink wine! let glasses clinking
Kill our cares and drown our thinking!
  Drink wine, beverage fine,

No maiden's eyes can rival its shine!
Happiness lies in a flagon of wine!

I trusted a friend whom I thought true, —
        Drink wine, brothers mine!
He played me false and robbed me too, —
        Drink wine! 't is this we 're drinking
Keeps our spirits up from sinking!
        Drink wine, beverage fine!
Friendship nor love were e'er half so divine;
Happiness lies in a flagon of wine!

My houses and lands, both park and moor, —
        Drink wine, brothers mine!
Have passed away and left me poor, —
        Drink wine! 't is this we 're drinking
Kills all care and stops all thinking!
        Drink wine, beverage fine!
Brighter than gold is its glimmering shine:
Happiness lies in a flagon of wine!

AN AUTOBIOGRAPHY.

I WAS born some time ago, but I know not
why:
I have lived, — I hardly know either how or
where:
Some time or another, I suppose, I shall die;
But where, how, or when, I neither know nor
care!

AT THE CIRCUS.

ACROSS the stage, with its blaze of lights,
From fly to fly in the heated air
A slack rope hung, and in spangled tights
Sat "Signor" somebody swinging there.

Now he swung by a single arm ;
Now by a single leg swung he ;
A fall had done him a grievous harm,
He balanced and turned so recklessly.

I watched awhile. "It is well," I said,
"If people want reckless feats, it is well.
The tickets are bought, the money is paid,
And 't were more of a show if he but fell."

I turned away : he was swinging yet :
And I glanced on the crowded house around, —

Boxes, circle, and wide parquette
  Breathlessly watching, without a sound.

In a 'graceful pose, on a cushioned seat,
  I saw Her sitting, to gaze at the man.
You could almost have heard my poor heart beat,
  With the riotous blood that through it ran.

There she sat, with her splendid eyes
  Fixed on the fellow so earnestly,
With more of the interest I should prize
  Than ever she gave in a glance to me.

Every time that he balanced and turned,—
  O, but her eyes grew large and shone,
Her bosom heaved and her fair cheek burned:
  To me she had been like a block of stone.

This poor, pitiful circus man,
  Swinging each night for his daily bread,
Had moved her more, since his act began,
  Than I could, stretched on my dying-bed.

Hollow, hollow, and false as hell!
  Love is a cheat, and life is a wreck!
What cared I if he swung or fell?
  What cared I if he broke his neck'?

DRINKING WINE.

POUR the mingled cream and amber!
  Let me drain the bowl again!
Such hilarious visions clamber
  Through the chambers of my brain.
Quaintest jests and queerest fancies
  Spring to life and fade away:
What care I how time advances?
  I am drinking wine to-day.

Here 's a motto terse and sentient,
  By it I will live and die!
Words of some rare tippling ancient,
  " Ever drunken, ever dry."
Fill again! let bubbles blind me!
  Sorrow, hide thy face away!

Satan, get thee hence behind me, —
  I am drinking wine to-day.

Cease thy prate of worldly glory,
  Cease thy prate of worldly gold !
I have heard that pleasant story
  Till it sounds a little old.
Let me drop such low ambitions ;
  Glory gnaws the heart away ;
Gold demands too stern conditions, —
  I am drinking wine to-day.

One more bowl — a goodly measure —
  Ere my merry mood be gone !
Wine's a feast of perfect pleasure, —
  Feast without a skeleton.
Love is false, and hope is waning ;
  Life a failure is alway !
Wine's the only good remaining, —
  Let me drain its lees to-day.

SONG OF THE SENSUOUS.

BRING me grapes, whose regal juice
  All my pent-up soul shall loose!
Bring me snow-crowned amber goblets,
  Overflown with liquid mirth!
  Let the night consume the day;
  Suns and moons pass swift away;
Let my life fade into pleasure;
  I am earthy, — of the earth!

  Let me choose myself a bride,
  Snowy-bosomed, dreamy-eyed;
Let our love to new expressions
  Every fleeting hour give birth!
  Locked in passion's close caress,
  Let us find forgetfulness!
What care I for aspirations?
  I am earthy, — of the earth!

Ye who list fame's trumpet-call,
Waste your lives and pleasures all;
When your eyes in death are glazing,
What are future glories worth?
Give me woman, wine, and sleep!
They who are in earnest weep:
Let me love and drink forever!
I am earthy, — of the earth!

QUAND MÊME.

I.

TWILIGHT is red in the west, and just where
the sun went down
Gleams a splendid halo, like that of a pictured
saint ;
The shadows of night fall fast, and purple the
moorlands brown,
While every passing moment the light in the
sky grows faint.
There are long dark lines of cloud that stretch
themselves in the west,
And tell of a bitter cold to come with the coming day,
And ever upon the wind there wails a voice of
unrest,
Wailing and soughing, sad and low, for the summer-time passed away.

II.

Glorious Summer! the pride, the queen of the
  livelong year ;.
 When insects chirp in the grass, and birds are
  carolling sweet ;
When the moors are gay with flowers, and the
  skies are diamond-clear,
 And the honeyed clover-blossoms breathe fragrance under our feet !
Here, on this selfsame moor, in a spirit of glad
  content,
 Humming, perchance, to myself, some fragment
  of musical rhyme,
Loitering, wandering idly, all careless whither I
  went, —
 Ah ! how oft have I walked, when the summer
  was in her prime !

III.

Well, I am walking now on the moorland, just
  as then,

But something has changed. Is it I ? or is it the
    whole wide world ?
Does anything ever change, outside of the hearts
    of men,
      Drifted about by their passions, and hither and
        thither whirled ?
I hum no snatches of rhyme, and a leaden weight
    of pain
      Burdens my gloomy spirit, and fevers my rest-
        less mind,
And I wander listless and slow, wantonly swinging
    my cane,
      Beating off the golden-rod tufts that rustle dry
        in the wind.

IV.

And still there rises before me, wherever I turn
    my gaze,
      The figure of her that I loved, when the summer
        was blossoming fair ;
A beautiful, haunting ghost, the love of my sun-
    nier days,

With her splendid, shadowy eyes, and her torrent of gleaming hair.
Lovely, loving, and loved! I remember every
caress,
Every word of endearment, and every gesture
and tone ;
Even her light, quick footstep, the rustling of her
dress,
Come to waken the olden thought as I walk on
the moor alone!

v.

Well, thank God! it is over, and naught but the
ghost abides ;
I have cast her forth forever, and sealed the
gates of my heart!
My pulse beats calmly now, as the flowing of
ocean tides ;
And I know that love is but madness, and
wisdom the better part:
For just as a woman is fair, so is she false
alway ;

She is vain, and the flatterer wins where the
    earnest man is scoffed ;
Give her but praise and folly, be idle, flippant, and
    gay,
And just in a due proportion, as your will—so
    her heart — is soft !

VI.

O, how I scorn myself, that I should be juggled
    and fooled,
    Vowing and promising love to an idle-minded
      girl ;
Degrading my very manhood, to find, when my
    blood had cooled,
    That she had lent me a tawdry cheat, where I
      had given a pearl !
She, — how well she could smile, while her heart
    was a lump of ice ;
    Kiss me, and sharpen a dagger to deal me a
      deadly blow ;
Weave garlands of fairest blossoms, to deck me, a
    sacrifice ;

And call me her dearest friend, while she was
    my dearest foe!

VII.

High in the heavens above stretch threatening
    hands of cloud,
  And a muttered malediction is whispered now
    on the breeze;
Thus do I stretch my hands, and curse the fickle
    and proud;
  Thus do I curse from my inmost heart all lovely
    liars like these!
'T is the brand of the eldest mother; the cause of
    the fall of man;
  We are weak and foolish, and eat of any fruit
    she may give;
And so I curse them all, who still, since the world
    began,
  Have smilingly poisoned our hearts until we are
    loath to live!

VIII.

O, may the wrath of Heaven — But hold, — I
    am rash, just now :
  Would I really wring her soul, and bring her to
    sharp despair ?
Wrinkle with heavy sorrow that beautiful, tranquil
    brow,
  And mingle silvery threads in the shining gold
    of her hair ?
No : I would rather choose that she might repent
    her wrong,
  With a softened sadness, born of this she has
    brought to me ;
The woman, after all, is not so sturdy and strong
  As we, and we should forgive, if we would for-
    given be.

IX.

Then, perchance, in the light that repentance
    sometimes shows,
  She could see this cross I bear, and pity my
    weary lot,

Till, in a gentler moment, touched deep by these
     cruel woes,
  Her heart — it was always kind — might yield
     once more ; why not ?
Ah, could it only be !   What joy would I not give
     up,
  To know that my form again in its olden shrine
     were set !
That again the wine of life could flash in the
     jewelled cup —
  O heart of mine ! what is this ?   More than
     ever I love her yet !

AT NEWPORT.

[A FRAGMENT.]

I WALKED on Newport's frowning rocks one
    day,
Watching the breakers' feathery lines of spray
Dash sternly up against the boulders there,
To fall away in nothingness and air, —
Just as we mortals, hopeful and elate,
Dash ourselves into nothing, against fate:
And — as we mourn to find our efforts lost —
The fretted surf, in frothy turmoil tossed,
Made melancholy moan, and seemed to tell
How brightly hope arose, how soon it fell.

Thus musing, I, in philosophic mood,
Was led upon man's littleness to brood,
And marvelled if he ever gains the prize
Which seems most worthy to his longing eyes....

We toil for wealth, till, prematurely old,
We lose all taste for joys that come of gold.
We labor hard for fame, and find at last
That glory comes not till the grave is past ;
We sigh for leisure, but to learn, too late,
That heavy *ennui* is its wedded mate.

' It is the world,' I said, ' has gone astray ;
My star has risen on a thankless day.
Not now, as once, where swords are girded on,
Can victors triumph when the field is won.
The shout of conquering armies must arise
Only when death has glazed the hero's eyes,
And the good news of victory smite his ear
Only, alas ! when he has ceased to hear.
Bravest of all, he dies and never knows
Whether his friends have triumphed, or his foes.

' I will have none of this. I will forswear
The world, its feverish hope, its feverish care.
The student's toil is vacant of reward
As his who carves a future with his sword.

Let those who may find joy in dusty books,
Stagnate in alcoves, dessicate in nooks
Where dust and bigotry hold rival reigns,
And scholars fill their heads with dead men's
    brains !
I will not waste my life from youth to age
To leave my name upon a title-page.

' And so in all things Fate is most unjust.
Beauty itself is made of common dust.
The cynic's sneer was hardly less than true, —
Love is, indeed, but ' selfishness for two.'
Where Venus once with Hymen held her court,
Young men are bartered and young maids are
    bought,
Unholy lips breathe forth unholy vows ;
And fading blossoms droop on faded brows.
So, till some purer life than this I see,
No nuptial garland shall be twined for me.

' I will not mingle with my fellow-men,
To be deceived and to deceive again.

Call me ascetic, cynic, what you will,
I shall be calm and philosophic still,
And, all unheeding what the world may say,
Will not bow down to idols made of clay.
I care not for the verdict of the crowd.
Shame cannot crush, nor honor make me proud,
The while in perfect peace I dwell apart,
True to myself and tranquil in my heart.

' What matters honor and what matters shame ?
A hundred years — and all will be the same.
Hence with the earthy idol and its throne, —
And let me walk forgotten and alone,
Where dancing mist and flying foam arise,
And distant seas commune with distant skies ;
Where slanting drives the white-winged ocean bird,
And naught save thunderous breakers can be heard,
Or solemn sounds of gusty winds that roar
Down the gray stretches of a ghostly shore.' ...

Thus, with the billows' murmur in my ear,
I was not conscious of a footstep near,

And, self-communing in my solitude,
Saw not a figure that before me stood —
Until a girl-voice, sweet as silver bells,
Rang out, "O come, and help me gather shells!"...
In dire retreat my gloomy fancies fled ;
The train of thought was lost: I raised my
    head, —
And met a Fate against whose rosy chain
Philosophers philosophize in vain.

There, sharply drawn against a pearly sky,
I saw a face half merry and half shy,
With shadowy eyes and mouth of perfect mould,
And hair of softest brown inmixed with gold.
A slender figure, full of gentle grace,
Matched the rare beauty of the girlish face :
And to my eye the apparition seemed
Something an artist lover might have dreamed,
After a day of earnest strife with art,
To reproduce the darling of his heart.

*   *   *   *   *

GLORIA.

[IN TIME OF WAR.]

THE laurels shine in the morning sun,
   The tall grass shakes its glittering spears,
And the webs the spiders last night spun
   Are threaded with pearly tears.

At peace with the world and all therein,
   I walk in the fields this summer morn:
What should I know of sorrow or sin,
   Among the laurels and corn?

But, hark! through the corn a murmur comes —
   'T is growing — 't is swelling — it rises high —
The thunder of guns and the roll of drums,
   And an army marching by.

Away with the sloth of peace and ease!
   'T is a nation's voice that seems to call.

Who cares for aught, in times like these,
   Save to win — or else to fall!

Farewell, O shining laurels, now!
   I go with the army marching by :
Your leaves, should I win, may deck my brow,
   Or my bier, if I should die.

CAMP COGITATIONS.

[IN TIME OF WAR.]

I.

THE moon is riding, full, behind the black
and naked trees,
Like a redly blazing beacon on the horizon it
gleams;
And the swaying cedar branches sigh more
sadly in the breeze;
And a hoarser voice is calling from the angry
mountain streams;
In the dusk the snowy tents of my companions
fade away:
Rocky crags loom high above me, purple shadows round me fall,
And I hear the clang of weapons, and the hungry chargers' neigh,
And the measured tramp of colûmns, and the
evening bugle-call.

II.

Eighteen centuries have fleeted since upon the
    earth there came
One who taught the creed of kindness, of for-
    giveness, and of peace,
One who bade us love our neighbor in the
    Heavenly Father's name :
Yet the god of battle riots, and his temples still
    increase.
For the ancient evil lingers ; man has war
    within his soul,
So he loves the clash and carnage, and the wild,
    triumphal shout :
Right and wrong against each other strive with-
    in him for control ;—
Ah, the ancient evil lingers, and he fain must
    fight it out.

III.

I, who dwell in scenes of warfare, may I not
    be something dulled

To the finer shades of justice, to the nicer sense
    of right?
I, who only do my thinking when the battle's
    storm has lulled,
And there comes a time of quiet, as upon this
    wintry night.
Can we, do we, settle questions, who is right
    and who is wrong,
By the shock of rushing squadrons and the leaden
    hail and rain?
Is there really then a judgment in the wild,
    unearthly song
Of the rifled-cannon bullet as it hurtles o'er
    the slain?

IV.

Ah, the finest-drawn philosophy must fall before
    the truth;
And the truth is plain and simple, as we own
    with one accord;
When the foe is at our thresholds hoary age
    and callow youth,

Leaving argument and reason, trust sublimely
    to the sword ;
And the student and the thinker, when the bat-
    tle is at hand,
When the monster glares before them, seek to
    bandy words no more ;
But a splendid fury rises, overwhelming all the
    land,
And a nation's voice is lifted in the symphony
    of war !

V.

So the thinkers who determine all the ways of
    Deity, —
All His wondrous means of working out the
    wisely hidden end, —
The philosophers who think to make us think
    that they can see
How the plans of God are laid, and whither-
    ward His labors tend, —
These may sigh, and say the present is no bet-
    ter than the past,

These may call us savage creatures, who appeal
to shot and shell;
But the truth remains triumphant, and our armies
gather fast,
And who meets his death in battle be assured
he meets it well.

VI.

Man must be the thing he is; he must express
himself in deeds;
So this outward war expresses only that which
wars within.
Do you, planting crimson roses, look for lilies
from their seeds?
No! a nation without war must be a nation
without sin.
If the hilt is in the hand, 't is surely there the
hilt belongs;
Man and man are aye in conflict; call it war
or what you will:
All the world is full of lies, — of old and thickly
crusted wrongs, —

And when blood is boiling hotly, there is always
    blood to spill.

VII.

See, the moon has risen high above the black
    and naked trees,
Like a shield of burnished silver on the sky of
    night it gleams;
Comes the sighing of the cedars ever sadly on
    the breeze;
Comes the sound of falling* waters from the
    troubled mountain streams.
Sternly frown the crags above me; darker shad-
    ows round me fall,
And the fires of the encampment flash and
    smoulder fitfully....
If the foeman break our slumber, ere the morn-
    ing bugle-call,
Is the victor's goodly laurel, or the cypress
    wreath for me?

JUNE 24, 1859.

I SEE the surf on Sandy Hook;
   I see the bay below me spread;
And here I lie, with pipe and book,
   And the blue sky overhead.

A quarter of a century
   Has passed, and still I live to say
(Ah, little joy it gives to me!)
   "I'm twenty-five to-day."

It is not very long to live;
   At twenty-five we're scarcely men;
And yet, a trifle I would give
   If 't were threescore and ten.

A dozen threads among my hair
   Have changed from chestnut-brown to snow;

But if they paled from weight of care
  It had been long ago.

About my eyes and on my brow
  A few faint wrinkles I can trace;
Time sets his signet even now
  Upon my form and face.

And yet I look both young and fresh;
  I am not worn, nor pale, nor thin;
Care's scars are slight upon the flesh,
  But deep on that within.

Ah yes! as seasons onward roll
  My outward form seems still to thrive;
But, looking back, I fear my soul
  Is more than twenty-five.

JUNE 24, 1864.

I 'M thirty : 't is not very old :
    Yet never younger shall I be ;
Nor do I care my youth to hold :
    'T is not so very dear to me.

True, I have lived my share of life,
    And found me many goodly friends ;
But, with all this, enough of strife,
    And toil, and loss, to make amends.

And all my joys have wedded been
    With bitter griefs : alas ! the bell
That rings to-day the marriage in,
    To-morrow tolls the funeral knell.

Yet, though my brightest hopes have paled,
    My faith in future good holds fast ;
My strength and courage have not failed,
    And all shall finish well at last !

II.

GAY.

" I do enjoy this bounteous, beauteous earth,
And dote upon a jest."
                              HOOD.

" He was full of joke and jest,
But all his merry quips are o'er."
                              TENNYSON.

DON LEON'S BRIDE.

A TALE OF THE CARNIVAL.

I.

'TWAS — let 's see — ever so long ago,
   There lived in Madrid, as you must know,
A gay cavalier
Who ne'er
Knew a fear
Of the doughtiest kind of a masculine foe;
   And who loved the ladies
   Of Seville and Cadiz
     As well as he did
     Those of Madrid, —
Indeed, I won't swear that he did n't hanker,
At times, for the girls of Salamanca.
   Yet still, in spite of his love and care
   For the sparkling eyes and the raven hair,

He had n't the luck

(Or, it may be, the pluck,

Though 't was hardly worth daring what he

did n't dare), —

In short, his affections he never had carried —

In having what young women call "an affair" —

So far as to think much about getting married.

He drank and he fought

Far more than he ought ;

And the records say

That, by night or day,

He cut up such shines, and in such a way,

That the daily papers,

Describing his capers,

Declared him the gayest of all the gay.

So much for my hero ; I 'm thinking, though,

That you might like to know

His name ;

And that same

I 'll tell you at once ;

'T was Señor Don Leon de Bayaldefonse.

II.

'T is carnival-time,
  And many a chime
From silvery, clear-toned chapel-bells,
Is falling in sweet, melodious swells
    On the air of the soft Castilian clime.
  The stars are bright
  In the sky of night,
  And the moon is pouring her holy light
On grove, and garden, and plain, and steep.
    The wind, as it blows,
    Sings love to the rose,
And kisses the orange-blooms to sleep.
  There's life in the town,
  For, up and down,
A hurrying, countless, jovial throng
Is surging along,
  And the gentle pulses of music beat
  In time to the tread of the dancers' feet ;
The colored lamps swing to and fro,
Casting a myriad-tinted glow
On the masked and motley crowd below,

Like the varied hues of the bow of hope,
Or those of a mammoth kaleidoscope.

III.

Don Leon is there,
With vivacious air,
Costumed and masked with scrupulous care, —
      Dancing and singing,
      Love-glances flinging,
   Stealing sly kisses
   From indiscreet misses,
Whispering to them in a corner alone,
Guessing their names without telling his own,
   Showering praises
   On them and their graces,
   Lifting their masks from their beautiful faces,
      And playing such pranks,
      With all classes and ranks,
That every one sees, as plain as can be,
Who knows Señor Leon, that this must be he!...
   At length my gay hero a lady espies,
   So carefully veiled as to hide e'en her eyes ;

But her voice is so sweet,—
Such music complete,—
Her dress is so rich, yet so tasteful and neat,—
So bewitching he finds her, in air and demeanor,
He 's almost in love, ere he hardly has seen her!

IV.

He speaks to this lady, and leads her aside,—
He earnestly begs her not to hide
Her beauties rare,
With such jealous care :
" For," says he, " I know that you must be fair !"
" Good sir," she answers, " my fate has said
That I must never, till I am wed,
Remove this mask ;
So do not ask,
But let us dance as we are, instead."
Her voice was low
As the winds that blow
O'er the hills where Aragon's roses grow,
And the songs that heavenly angels sing
No sweeter, purer, or clearer ring.

Don Leon turned him half away, —
He heard that voice, and naught could he say,
Although he 'd have given
His hopes of heaven
To have seen her face for a moment, even ;
  But to save all Spain
  From sorrow and pain,
  He could n't have asked her once again.
As the music arose
He drew her close,
And off they danced, on the tips of their toes,
  With many a fling,
  And many a swing,
  Whirling, twirling, shifting, swaying,
  Numberless pretty things softly saying,
    Darting along
    Through the mazy throng,
  Till poor Don Leon felt that he
  Was falling a victim to mystery,
And that it was true as heaven above
That he was heels-over-head in love !

V.

The waltz was done,
With its frolic and fun,
And the Don to plead his suit begun.
Again he led the lady aside,
To a lonely part of the courtyard wide,
And begged she would
Be kind and good
Enough, to take the veil from her hood;
But no, — she would n't, —
She said she could n't;
"Why not!" asked he;
" Because," said she,
" You 'd certainly be
Scared half to death with what you would see."
" I 'm not afraid,"
Don Leon said,
And his hand on the veil he gently laid:
" Back! back!" she cried,
Quite terrified,
" My face I must forever hide,

Until I am wedded, — a lawful bride!"
  Alas for the Don, —
  His heart was gone!
  'T was a solemn step to decide upon, —
A serious joke,
If the truth were spoke,
And very like " buying a pig in a poke " !
  But he 'd vowed to know, by hook or by crook,
  How the face of the charming one might look,
  So her hand he took,
  And swore by the book
That, if she was willing his heart to delight,
They would go and be married, that blesséd
      night!
  " Ah me ! " cried the lady, " at last I have found
  A man with true-hearted courage crowned ! "
  And she fell in his arms with a joyful bound.
Then off they went,
On a wedding bent,
As swift as a bolt from a cross-bow sent,
  Or (to be more modern), as swift as the bolt
  That 's sent from the pistols of Colonel Colt, —

And Father Ignacio Iago Malony
    Soon showed
    Them the road
To matrimony.

VI.

Now for the awful mystery !
The Don was almost dying to see
    The face of his wife,
    Yet a dreadful strife
Arose in his breast.
And it must be confessed
That he felt — well, terribly nervous, at best !
In a room, in the old baronial hall
That the Bayaldefonses, one and all,
Had owned since the time of Adam's fall,
    Stood the Don and his bride,
    Side by side,
Their hearts overflowing with love and pride.
    " Come, bare thy head,"
    The bridegroom said ;
" Fair lady mine,

Let the light divine
Beam forth from those beautiful eyes of thine !
    O, let me sip
    The dew of thy lip,
Or kiss the blush from thy peachy cheek !
O, haste, sweet wife, nor longer seek
    To keep thy glorious charms concealed, —
    Take off thy veil, — let them be revealed ! "
        She dropped the veil, —
        The Don turned pale, —
    His joy — his pleasure — his hope — was gone, —
He had lost, before he had fairly won :
O gentle reader, pity the Don, —
What *do* you suppose he looked upon ?...
Only a SKELETON !

THE BIG OYSTER.

'TWAS a hazy, mazy, lazy day,
    And the good smack *Emily* idly lay
Off Staten Island, in Raritan Bay,
      With her canvas loosely flapping.
The sunshine slept on the briny deep,
Nor wave nor zephyr could vigils keep,
The oystermen lay on the deck asleep,
      And even the cap'n was napping.

The smack went drifting down the tide —
The waters gurgling along her side —
Down where the bay grows·vast and wide —
      A beautiful sheet of water ;
With scarce a ripple about her prow,
The oyster-smack floated, silent and slow,

With Keyport far on her starboard bow,
    And South Amboy on her quarter.

But, all at once, a grating sound
Made the cap'n awake and glance around ;
" Hold hard !" cried he, "we've run aground,
    As sure as all tarnation !"
The men jumped up, and grumbled, and swore ;
They also looked, and plainly saw
That the *Emily* lay two miles from shore,
    At the smallest calculation.

Then, gazing over the side, to see
What kind of bottom this shoal might be,
They saw, in the shadow that lay to the lee,
    A sight that filled them with horror !
The water was clear, and beneath it, there,
An oyster lay in its slimy lair,
So big, that to tell its dimensions fair
    Would take from now till to-morrow.

And this it was made the grating sound ;
On this the *Emily* ran aground ;

And this was the shoal the cap'n found —
    Alack ! the more is the pity.
For straight an idea entered his head :
He 'd drag it out of its watery bed,
And give it a resting-place, instead,
    In some saloon in the city.

So, with crow, and lever, and gaff, and sling,
And tongs, and tackle, and roller, and ring,
They made a mighty effort to bring
    This hermit out of his cloister.
They labored earnestly, day and night, ·
Working by torch and lantern light,
Till they had to acknowledge that, do what they
      might
    They never could budge the oyster !

The cap'n fretted, and fumed, and fussed —
He swore he 'd " have that 'yster, or bust ! "
But, for all his oaths, he was quite nonplussed ;
    So, by way of variation,
He sat him quietly down, for a while,

To cool his anger and settle his bile,
And to give himself up, in his usual style,
    To a season of meditation.

Now, the cap'n was quite a wonderful man;
He could do almost anything any man can,
And a good deal more, when he once began
    To act from a clear deduction.
But his wonderful power — his greatest pride —
The feat that shadowed all else beside —
The talent on which he most relied —
    Was his awful power of suction!

At suction he never had known defeat!
The stoutest suckers had given in, beat,
When he sucked up a quart of apple-jack, neat,
    By touching his lips to the measure!
He'd suck an oyster out of its shell,
Suck shrimps or lobsters equally well;
Suck cider, till inward the barrel-heads fell —
    And seemed to find it a pleasure!

Well, after thinking a day or two,
This doughty sucker imagined he knew
About the best thing he could possibly do, ·
  To secure the bivalvular hermit.
" I 'll bore through his shell, as they bore for coal,
With an auger fixed on the end of a pole,
And then, through a tube, I 'll suck him out,
   whole —
  A neat little swallow, I term it!"

The very next day, he returned to the place
Where his failure had thrown him into disgrace ;
And there, with a ghastly grin on his face,
  Began his submarine boring.
He worked a week, for the shell was tough,
But reached the interior soon enough
For the oyster, who found such surgery rough —
  Such grating, and scraping, and scoring!

The shell-fish started, the water flew,
The cap'n turned decidedly blue,
But thrust his auger still further through,

To quiet the wounded creature.
Alas! I fear that my tale grows sad,
The oyster naturally felt quite bad,
And ended by getting excessively mad,
In spite of its peaceful nature.

It arose, and, turning itself on edge,
Exposed a ponderous shelly wedge,
All covered with slime, and seaweed, and sedge —
A conchological wonder !
This wedge flew open, as quick as a flash,
Into two great jaws, with a mighty splash ;
One scraunching, crunching, crackling crash —
And the smack was gone to thunder !

THE DRINKING OF THE APPLE–JACK.

COME, let us drink the apple-jack !
   Cut the tough lemon with the blade ;
Hot let the water then be made ;
There gently pour the liquor ; there
Sift the white sugar in with care,
   And mix them all as gingerly
As poets mingle rhythmic feet
To print in some æsthetic sheet :
   So mix we the apple-jack.

What drink we in the apple-jack ?
Buds, which the sprees of nights and days
Shall swell to blossoms all ablaze ;
Spots, where the rash, a crimson guest,
Shall put our good looks to the test.

We drink, from the distillery,
A balm for each ill-omened hour,
A pleasant alcoholic shower,
   When we drink the apple-jack.

What drink we in the apple-jack?
Sweets, from that Jersey farm, of Spring's,
That load the wagons, carts, and things,
When from the orchard-row he pours
His fruit to the distillery doors;
   And toddy-blossoms, red that be.
Drinks for the sick man's silent room,
For the *bon vivant* rosy bloom,
   We brew, with the apple-jack.

What drink we in the apple-jack?
Heads that shall swell in sunny June,
To ache like fun in the August noon,
And droop as sober folks come by
Under the blue September sky;
   And fellows, wild with noisy glee,

Shall breathe strong fragrance as they pass,
And tumble on the tufted grass —
  The effect of the apple-jack.

And when above this apple-jack
The silver spoons are quivering bright,
And songs go howling through the night,
We, whose young eyes o'erflow with mirth,
Shall quaff our punch by cottage-hearth,
  And guests in prouder homes shall see,
Beside the red blood of the grape,
A bottle of a different shape —
  The bottle of the apple-jack.

The glory of this apple-jack
Winds and our flag of stripe and star
Shall bear to coasts that lie afar,
Where men shall drink till all is blue
The apple-jack of Sandynew;
  And they who roam upon the sea
Shall mourn the past but happy day

When grog made labor seem like play,
　　The day of the apple-jack.

Each year shall give this apple-jack
A mellower taste, a warmer bloom,
A potency 'gainst mopes and gloom,
And make it, when the frost-clouds lower,
A thing for punch of wondrous power.
　　The years shall come and pass, but we
Shall grow no better where we lie,
While summer's songs and autumn's sigh
　　Shall ripen the apple-jack.

And time shall waste this apple-jack!
O, when its aged barrels grow
Light, as the rare old juice runs low,
Shall fraud and force and iron will
Oppress us with a Maine-law bill?
　　What shall the tasks of mercy be,
Amid the todless toper's tears,
If this should come, when length of years
　　Is wasting this apple-jack?

" Who barreled this old apple-jack ? "
The bibbers of that distant day
Thus to some aged Sport shall say ;
And, fingering his goblet's stem,
The gray-haired sage shall answer them :
  " A poet of Jersey fame was he,
Born in the heavy drinking times ;
'T is said he made some quaint old rhymes
  On drinking the apple-jack ! "

SINGLE AND DOUBLE.

A CHRISTMAS JINGLE.

I.

L AST Christmas, I remember,
  I sat beside the hearth,
And watched each glowing ember
  To tiny flames give birth,
While the snow-flakes of December
  Were whitening the earth.

Rapt close in meditation,
  And all that sort of thing,
The idle brain's creation
  And vague imagining,
I had a visitation
  Perhaps worth mentioning.

My pipe its clouds emitted
  In wreaths of azure hue,
Through which strange visions flitted,
  As they are wont to do
When one is sombre-witted
  And feels a little blue.

Strange vision! girls with faces
  Of loveliest blush and smile,
Whose forms wore all the graces
  That strengthen woman's wile,
When clothed in silks and laces
  Cut in the latest style.

Then rare, melodious noises,—
  Some seraphic trombone,—
Came mingling with sweet voices
  Blent in a tender tone,
Saying,—"When all the Earth rejoices,
  Why shouldst thou be here alone?"

I felt that I was weary
  Upon that Christmas day;

That I alone was dreary
  While others all were gay
With Christmas feasting cheery, —
  So I had n't much to say.

And again they put the query,
  Why I should lonely be
While other folks were merry,
  And said they could n't see
Why I should be so very
  Fond of my misanthropy.

While thus these figures fluttered
  My lonely hearthstone o'er,
And still these voices uttered
  Their question as before,
I, half unconscious, muttered
  "I 'll be alone no more!"

"Away with melancholy!
  I 'll seek me out a bride,
And when the berried holly
  Glows red at Christmas-tide,

I 'll know of no such folly
  As a lonely fireside!"

Then fled the fairy vision!
  Their object was attained;
They had fulfilled their mission,
  Their ultimatum gained:
They fled, but my decision
  Quite palpably remained.

II.

Again the Christmas season
  Rolls round as seasons roll;
The feast is more than reason,
  The flow is more than soul,
And tyrant Care, by treason,
  Is drowned in many a bowl.

Within my pleasant chamber
  I sit and muse once more,

While from the hearth each ember
    Gleams red across the floor
And snow-flakes of December
    Lie white on hill and shore.

Again I sit, but never
    As once I used to sit,
By phantoms haunted ever —
    Vague forms that fade and flit,
Enough to make a clever
    Fellow have a stupid fit.

Ah no! my resolution
    Has straightly been put through,
And another institution
    Has crept my life into.
I have declared for " Fusion,"
    And my ally has proved true!

My Ally, — that 's my Alice...
    A vision far more dear
Than those that rose in malice,
    From the pungent Latakia

That burned within the chalice
  Of my meerschaum pipe, last year.

No more in lonely musing
  I hear the slow hours chime;
No more my lot abusing
  In sentimental rhyme;
No more I 'm caught refusing
  To have a jolly time!

But, free from blues and bother,
  Quite cosily at ease,
I sit by Baby's mother
  With Baby on my knees,
And look from one to t' other
  As proudly as you please!

So you, who do as I did
  On Christmas-days gone by,
Ere She and I decided
  Our forces to ally,
If lonely you 've abided,
  This other method try!

Old bachelors grow spiteful,
　As I erst-while have known.
Heart-loneliness is frightful,
　And in the Book 't is shown
That it is n't good or rightful
　For man to be alone.

I hear my Alice singing
　As the Christmas snow-flakes fall,
And the Christmas-bells are ringing
　From every belfry tall,
This Christmas burthen bringing,
　" God bless us, one and all ! "

THE BALLAD OF FISTIANA.

MY form is wasted with my woe,
      Fistiana.
There is no fame for me below,
      Fistiana.
My fame has gone, like melted snow,
Though I can hit a heavy blow,
      Fistiana.
Alone I wander to and fro,
      Fistiana.

Once, my fame was widely growing,
      Fistiana;
Day and night my friends were crowing,
      Fistiana;
I was blowing, wine was flowing,

When I was to battle going,
          Fistiana.
But, alas! 't was naught but blowing,
          Fistiana.

In the ring, till almost night,
          Fistiana,
I stood proudly up in fight,
          Fistiana.
Although the blood bedimmed my sight,
With stars that glimmered swift and bright,
          Fistiana,
And left my eyes in shocking plight,
          Fistiana.

The umpire stood against the wall,
          Fistiana ;
He watched my fist among them all,
          Fistiana ;
He saw me fight; I heard him call:
My foeman was both strong and tall,
          Fistiana :

He pressed me close against the wall,
   Fistiana.

My heavy counter went aside,
   Fistiana,—
The false, false counter went aside,
   Fistiana, —
The curséd counter glanced aside;
I missed his nob : my blow was wide,
   Fistiana,—
My blow was very wild and wide,
   Fistiana!

O, narrow, narrow was the space,
   Fistiana!
Loud rang my backers' heavy bass,
   Fistiana.
O, deathful blows were dealt apace,
The battle deepened in its place,
   Fistiana ;
But I went down upon my face,
   Fistiana.

They should have sponged me where I lay,
 Fistiana ;
How could I rise and come away,
 Fistiana ?
How should I look, the second day?
They might have left me where I lay,
 Fistiana :
Bruised, mauled, and pounded into clay,
 Fistiana.

O feeble nose ! why didst thou break,
 Fistiana ?
O me ! so pale and limp and weak,
 Fistiana :
I took my drink, but could not speak,
With such a jaw and lip and cheek,
 Fistiana,
Where fists had played at hide-and-seek,
 Fistiana.

They cried aloud ; I heard their cries,
 Fistiana :

Their plaudits rent the very skies,
   Fistiana ;
I felt the tears and blood arise
Up from my heart into my eyes,
   Fistiana.
Who says there 's fun in fighting, lies,
   Fistiana.

O curséd hand ! O curséd blow !
   Fistiana !
Unhappy me, by it laid low,
   Fistiana !
All night my " claret " seemed to flow ;
I sat alone, in utter woe,
   Fistiana :
To fight again I 'll never go,
   Fistiana.

THE MODERN MITHRIDATES.

HO! bring my breakfast! give to me
    Bread that is snowy and light of weight, —
Of alum and bone-dust let it be,
    Chalk, and ammonia's carbonate :
Sulphates of zinc and copper too,
    Plaster of Paris, finely ground,
Will make it evenly white, clear through,
    With the outside nicely browned.

Give me butter to eat with the bread, —
    Colored with saffron and turmeric,
Or orpiment, richer in tint 't is said ;
    Let lard and sheep's brains make it thick.
Give me tea of a clear green hue,
    Made of soapstone, and willow-leaves,
Arsenite of copper and Prussian blue, —
    Their flavor the palate deceives.

Bring sugar, and sweeten the potion well, —
  Sugar of lead, and iron, and sand,
Sweet as honey of Hydromel,
  Or the pressure of Mithridates' hand!
Though maybe coffee would clear my head
  Better than such a cup of tea, —
Coffee of ochre, Venetian red,
  And the potent chicory.

Then, with my chop, let pickles green
  Cool my tongue with flavorous bliss;
Steeped and soaked, they must have been,
  In salts of copper and verdigris:
Most inviting to me they are
  When full of the pungent taste I find
In sulphuric acid vinegar, —
  A condiment just to my mind.

Ha! you start! you think that I,
  Being a man of mortal clay,
After my meal will surely die,
  For these are deadly poisons, you say:

Poisons? yes! yet one and all
    Are found on every grocer's shelves;
Our bills of mortality are not small,
    But how can we help ourselves?

PATTI.

PATTI is going away!   The columned hall
    Of the Academy shall miss her voice.
No more may painted dome and panelled wall
Ring to the silvery sweetness we heard fall
    From her fair lips, to make our hearts rejoice!

A glittering triumph may await her where
    The sea rolls up its foam on Albion's shore,
And noble heads may bow before her there;
But those pure notes that floated down the air
    Of Irving Place shall greet our ears no more!

No doubt, she goes to study and to sing;
    No doubt, she goes to win a lasting name;
No doubt her praises through the world will ring,
And she will wed a Count, or some such thing,
    With lots of money, and a dreadful name!

·

But who, ah, who will take the vacant place
  She leaves within our hearts, when she is gone?
That childlike purity, that girlish grace,
That fresh, fair voice, and ever gentle face,
  Our tenderest love and sympathy have won!

Well, since it must be so, O, let us lift
  A prayer that she may prosper and rejoice;
That, in the voyage of life, her bark may drift
Safe through the storms that beat and winds that
    shift,
  Steered by the goodly compass of her voice!

1860.

PICCOLOMINI.

" We understand M'dlle Piccolomini's engagements terminate in March, and that she will then leave the stage, in accordance with the wish of her family." — *London Paper.*

FAREWELL, thou bon-bon of the lyric stage:
    Thou wert divine, the rest are only clever;
None else my thirst for music can assuage.
    Farewell, sweet singing little one, forever!

Thou goest from triumphs, from a world of friends;
    Thou goest from present sweets, from future
        laurels,
Thou goest from all that heaven to genius
        sends, —
    Fêtes, gifts, loves, gloves, posters, footlights, and
        quarrels.

Thou hadst the grace, the winning way, the style,
    Thy face was full of fun, thy form was natty;

O, ne'er on earth shall I forget the smile
  That arched thy brow while singing "Batti,
      batti!"

Henceforth, when sorrowing and sad I sit
  Amid the buzz and glare and viol's ringing,
I 'll make me an ideal, and worship it, —
  I 'll fancy that I hear thee always singing.

So farewell, bon-bon of the lyric stage,
  Since family desires have power to sever
The world and thee.   I drop upon this page
  One tear, in bidding thee farewell forever.

1860.

THE DANGERS OF BROADWAY.

BY A PROMENADER.

I.

WITH a slam, and a smash, and a rattling
crash,
Come the sticks,
And the bricks,
Bits of glass, blind, and sash,
That the laborers rash
Tumble down, all the day,
From the houses now being torn down in Broadway.
Strange odors and musty,
The air sharp and dusty
With lime and with sand,
That no one can stand,
Make the street quite impassable,
The people irascible,

Till every one cries,
　　As he trembling goes,
With the sight of his eyes
　　And the scent of his nose
Quite stopped — or at least, much diminished,
" Gracious ! when will this city be finished ! "

II.

Mr. Smith builds a store — may be more —
　　In the year '53.
　　But, in '58, he
Finds that, which he calls " the old (!) building,"
　　a bore,
　　A disgrace to the town —
　　So of course it comes down,
　　And another, much stronger,
　　Goes up in its place,
　　With a handsomer face,
To last five years more, or perhaps a year longer.
　　Meanwhile Mr. Brown
　　Pulls down
His building, near by,

And the dust that he makes
Causes all sorts of aches ;
For, like his " improvements," 't is all in one's eye !

III.

But the dust's not the worst of this ruin accurst ;
'T is the danger,
Each stranger
(And citizen too) is always put through,
In walking amid such a hullabaloo.
E'en a temperance man —
Let him do all he can —
Is likely to get (and be well off at that)
An exceedingly heavy great brick in his hat.
Powdered with mortar,
Sprinkled with water,
Smoked, soaked,
Poked, choked,
Turned into the street,
By walks incomplete,
Till the pleasures of Broadway are sadly diminished,
And all say, "O gracious! when will it be finished?"

THE FOURTH OF JULY IN TOWN.

[Being the Lament of a Poet who could n't get away. The reader will observe that each verse is concluded by an explosive refrain, from the firearms without.]

I REALLY don't know what to do
  ('T was thus a Poet sang)
Amid this dreadful hubaboo
  That drives me crazy —
          (*Bang !*)

I did not wish in town to stay ;
  It cost me quite a pang
To find I could n't get away,
  But fate is cruel —
          (*Bang !*)

The streets are filled with smoke and noise,
  And everywhere a gang

Of ruffian men and rowdy boys
  Are firing pistols —
               (Bang !)

Ah! out of town the air is sweet,
  Where nodding roses hang
Above the brook that laves their feet,
  But here 't is horrid —
               (Bang !)

In every public place and hall
  The orators harangue,
Amid a dun and dusky pall
  Of smoke and sulphur —
               (Bang !)

Whatever patriots may say,
  With all their buncombe slang,
In town, this Independence Day
  Is but a nuisance —
               (Bang !)

'T was well enough, when into birth
Our Independence sprang;
But this! 't is Tophet here on earth —
   (Crack! crash!! whang!!!
   clang!!!! slam-bang!!!!!)

THE SHARPSHOOTER'S LOVE.

THE finest friend I ever knew,
　　And one with whom I dare not trifle;
Who in all danger sees me through,
Whose aim is ever good and true,
　　Is my sweet Minie Rifle.

She gently rests upon my arm,
　　Is always ready, always willing;
And though, in general, somewhat calm,
Wakes up, upon the first alarm,
　　To show she can be killing.

And she is very fair to see,
　　The most fastidious fancy suiting;
Her Locks are bright as they can be,
And that her Sight is good, to me
　　Is just as sure as shooting.

Though used to many a fiery spark,
    She's never careless in her pleasure;
She always aims to hit the mark,
And when her voice the Southrons hark,
    They find she's no Secesher.

The heaviest Load seems not to weigh
    Upon her more than 't were a trifle;
She's highly polished: and I'd pray,
Were I bereft of friends this day,
    O, leave me Minie Rifle!

THE SONG OF THE STONE-HULK.

TIME was I roved the Northern seas,
  To chase the blubbering whale,
But now I lie in dreamy ease
To rest my poor old ribs and knees.
  A Cell, but not a Sail.

A number of us calmly lie, —
  J. D. is not alone, —
And barristers who southward hie
Can comment, passing Charleston by,
  Upon the works of Stone.

Though old, I still am stanch and stout;
  A store of Rocks have I;
My comrades and myself, no doubt,
With such a lot of bars about,
  Will ne'er get high and dry.

The sharks, the porgies, and the whales
　Swim by with look intent,
And ask if, when I bent my sails
To lead the life this job entails,
　I followed out that bent.

Though Davis, spite of shame and sin,
　Controls the South, 't is true,
To Lincoln I my faith give in...
As I a three-master have been
　Two masters will not do.

When cannon against Sumter's wall
　Shall roar in warlike sort,
I 'll think, as howl the shot and ball
From frigates trim and taut and tall,
　'T is their, but not my, forte.

So here in Charleston Bay I lie,
　A part of war's great game;
To pass me let no skipper try,
For though he reck but little, I
　Shall wreck him all the same!

TWO SENSIBLE SERENADES.

I.

I SING beneath your lattice, Love,
  A song of great regard for you:
The moon is getting rather high;
    My voice is, too.

The lakelet in deep shadow lies,
Where frogs make much hullabaloo;
I think they sing a trifle hoarse,
    And, Love, me too.

· The blossoms on the pumpkin-vine
Are weeping diamond tears of dew;
'T is warm: the flowers are wilting fast;
    My linen too.

All motionless the cedars stand,
With silent moonbeams slanting through ;
The very air is drowsy, Love,
    And I am too.

O, could I soar on loving wings,
And at your window gently woo !
But then your lattice you would bolt —
    So I 'll bolt too.

And now I 've done my serenade,
Farewell ! my best regards to you ;
I 'll close with one (French) word for all,
    And that is tout.

II.

THE surf upon the distant shore is breaking ;
    Bright tears of dew the roses seem to weep ;
But you are prejudiced against awaking,
    So I 'll sing small, and let you have your sleep !
        Sleep, lady, sleep !

You shall not chide me for this song, love, shall
    you?
 I take great pains my voice subdued to keep,
For well I understand the lofty value
 All sane folks set upon a wholesome sleep.
    Sleep, lady, sleep!

Some fellows — at their nonsense oft I wonder —
 Sing out with voices strong, and loud, and deep,.
Until their loved ones wish they 'd go to thunder,
 Or, like myself, sing small, and let them sleep.
    Sleep, lady, sleep!

The grass is wet; I find that I am sneezing;
 This kind of thing is getting rather "steep";
The thought of rheumatism is n't pleasing,
 So, with your leave, I 'll home to bed and sleep.
    Sleep, lady, sleep!

NO MORE.

THE Summer Season 's over;
    No more I haunt the Springs or Shores;
No more I lie in clover,
    And suffer myriad rural bores.

I feel no headache warning
    Of sunstroke, 'neath the skies of fire;
I dance no more, till morning,
    With mortal maids who must perspire.

No more I haunt the stables,
    To learn how racing matters go;
No more I sleep on tables,
    Because " the house is crowded so."

No more the milk and honey
    Of watering-place cuisines are mine;

But I, for much less money,
  Can much more comfortably dine.

No more the famous waters
  Disgust my taste and make me ill;
No marriageable daughters
  Are now thrust at me, will or nill.

Sweet blondes, and brunettes haughty,
  No more with spangled tradesmen flirt;
No more their nags (2.40)
  Dash by, and cover me with dirt.

The dread mosquito, singing,
  No more torments me with his ways;
Nor, sharper tortures bringing,
  The still more terrible punaise.

The sea its rocks is scathing,
  As heretofore; but beauty bright
No more goes in a-bathing,
  In togs that render her a fright!

I see no white sails dotting
　　Old ocean's bosom, blue and broad:
I go no more a-yachting,
　　And lose my dinner — overboard.

Bluffed, badgered, bored, and bandied,
　　No more am I: I 'm home at last;
And own up — to be candid —
　　I 'm very glad the season 's past.

THE COMMON COUNCILMAN.

'TWAS an illegant Common Councilman,
  His nose it was red an' his eyes was
    sunken.
As grocery-clerk his life began,
  Till he had to "resign" for bein' dhrunken ;
'T was then he was thick widh the market
    boys,
  An' many an evenin' he got a singein',
Or helped to make confusion an' noise,
  At work on a blazin' roof, or an ingin'.

He managed the votes of his pet masheen,
  An' swep' his ward like a reg'lar hurricane ;
An' whin he was spacheless widh bog-poteen,
  He thanked the Lord he was no American !
So they 'lected him, aisy enough ;
  He could n't be Prisident — more 's the pity —

On account of the " Native American " stuff;
    But they giv' him a fat berth undher the city.

His hair was red and his brogue was nate,
    An' whin he 'rranged the affairs o' the na-
        tion,
His vote was always appropriate,
    For he voted for ivery appropriation :
Of blarney he had enough an' to shpare;
    His spache was wondherful fine an' flowery;
He was mighty fluent upon the swear,
    An' he kep' a " sample-room " in the Bowery.

Soon he came to belong to "the Ring,"
    An' got mighty rich widh his jobs an' leases,
Had horses an' wagins an' iverything,
    An' chucked his money around like Crœsis.
Ivery mornin' he rode in his shay,
    And went to Delmonico's for a luncheon ;
An' he drownded the shamrock St. Patrick's
        day
In a punch that fairly filled a puncheon.

All the relations he iver knew,
  To his wife's fourth cousin and great-aunt's
    brother,
Got a place undher the City too—
  Ivery wan had some pickins or other;
An' so he lived, respicted by all,
  Who, through him, could touch the City's
    rhino;
Whin he died, 't was an illegant funeral,
  An' he went—O, bother! it's more than I
    know.

THE CONSERVATIVE'S LAMENT.

(AFTER TENNYSON.)

I HATE the dreadful nigger, within the pile
    of wood ;
His name is the demagogue's weapon, dabbled
    with blood in its sheath ;
At Harper's Ferry still lingers a silent horror
    of blood,
    And Echo there, whatever is asked her, an-
    swers "death."

    For there is a ghastly grin on political faces
    found ;
The nigger is all their life — they know how to
    manage him well —
Dandled and flattered first, then crushed on po-
    litical ground —
    This is the rock on which the Whig Party
    split and fell.

Have we flung ourselves down? If so, the
    greatest of nations has failed;
Our honest men mutter and madden, our states-
    men are wan with despair;
When the nigger has walked through the land,
    the working classes have wailed,
    And the flying gold of the ruined merchants
    gleamed on the air.

I remember the time when my bitterest bile
    was stirred
By the *Herald's* gas, and the dead-weight *Times*,
    and the *Tribune's* fright,
When its white-coat editor said, in every col-
    umn, he heard
    The shrill-edged shriek of Kansas divide the
    shuddering night.

Villany somewhere? whose? I think they are
    villains all;
Not one politician his honest fame has main-
    tained;

And that old man, now lord of the White House
reception-hall,
  Will soon drop off from his term, and leave
us flaccid and drained.

Why do we prate of our government's power?
we have made it a curse—
  Pickpockets, each hand lusting for gold that
is not its own;
And the lust of gain, or the senator's cane, are
they better or worse
  Than the scalping done by the savage, in war,
with a sharpened stone?

But these are the days of advance, the works
of the men of mind,
  When who but a fool would have faith in a
politician's word?
Is it peace or war? ... civil war, as I think;
and that of a kind
  The viler as being political — abuse instead
of the sword.

Sooner or later I too may passively take the hint
Of the golden bribe — why not ? I have nei-
ther hope nor trust ;
May make myself eligible, set my face as a flint,
Cheat, be elected, and steal : who knows ? we
are ashes and dust.

March, 1860.

QUEER WEATHER.

THE summer is hot and the summer is dry,
　　The water is low in the stagnant pool;
There's a parching earth and a cloudless sky,
　　And even the cucumbers can't keep cool:
Still worse — while the summer astonishes all,
I fear there'll be very queer weather this fall.

In Dixie the thunder is fearfully loud,
　　The lightning is common, too, yonder, they say,
And e'en in the North is a gathering cloud
　　That may do us harm before clearing away:
It won't come amiss, then, to look for a squall,
And prepare for some very queer weather this fall.

'T is odd that while drouth scorches forest and plain,
　　And the land is as dry as an empty cup,
Poor Washington's troubled with too much reign,

And the people are praying the Pumps may
      dry up :
For change in the programme they earnestly call,
And I think they 'll have very queer weather
      this fall.

There 's a sprout in that city — a flourishing
      weed —
   That grows upon ruins and blooms on despair ;
It sucks up the richness that other plants need,
   And takes to itself all the sunshine and air ;
At present 't is lusty and thrifty and tall,
But I think 't will have very queer weather this fall.

Well, let us hope on, though the heavens may
      frown ;
   Such weather can hardly last always, you know ;
The day must come, even to Washington town,
   When the ruin-born blossoms no longer can blow ;
And sunshine shall follow, in cottage and hall,
The very queer weather that 's coming this fall !

FACILIS DECENSUS AVENUE.

["We see that one of our fashionable tailors has broken ground in Fifth Avenue, and converted one of the fine mansions therein into a magazine of garments. In a short time we may expect to see most of the magnificent private residences in this avenue. converted into retail stores and shops." — *Daily Newspaper*.]

I.

ACCORDING to popular talk,
The palatial street of New York
Is falling from grace
At a terrible pace.
I hear, when I promenade there,
Strange voices of grief in the air;
And I fancy I see
The sad sisters three,
With their black trailing dresses
And dishevelled tresses,
Go, solemn and slow,
To and fro,
In their woe,

Sighing,
And crying
" Eheu! Eheu! Eheu!
There 's a Tailor in Fifth Avenue!"

.

II.

O, sorry and sad was the day
When this Tailor came up from Broadway,
With his stitches,
And breeches,
His shears and his goose,
And his fashions profuse,
To the house that has been,
In years I have seen,
Most aristocratic
From basement to attic!
But gone are the flush and the fair,
And those voices still float in the air,
Sighing,
And crying
" Eheu! Eheu! Eheu!
There 's a Tailor in Fifth Avenue."

III.

Where sweet Crinolina once slept,
The sempstresses, may be, are kept;
And, perhaps, in her dressing-room, where
Her maid combed that glistening hair,
    Some cross-legged fellow,
    Round-shouldered and yellow,
May sit, with his needle and thread;
For the glory that reigned there has fled!
    How oft to that door she ascended
    When the ball or the party was ended,
      Flushed, beautiful, bright,
      A queen of delight,
An angel quite worthy of heaven!
To that door now a tailor's cart's driven.
No wonder that voice cries — "Eheu!
There's a Tailor in Fifth Avenue!"

IV.

Then where shall the flush and the fair
Find refuge? Ah, Echo says "Where?"
There are dentists in Madison Square;

The boarding-house, too, appears there;
    And I 've heard,
    In a word,
That some kind of factory, or mill,
Is soon to disturb Murray Hill!
    Now, if fashion must be
    (And it seems so to me)
    Crowded upward, each year,
    I very much fear
They 'll be shoved — and the thought makes
    me shiver —
Off the island and into the river;
    Sighing,
    And crying
  "Eheu! Eheu! Eheu!
There 's a Tailor in Fifth Avenue."

THE SONG OF THE HOME GUARD.

" LET dogs delight to bark and bite,"
  I have no taste for war ;
My joy is not in fire and fight,
In cannon's roar and bullet's flight,
  And nasty pools of gore.

O no, I hold 't is very wrong
  My fellow-man to slay ;
But when I see the martial throng
Go clattering by, ten thousand strong,
  I 'm carried quite away.

I love the drums' and trumpets' crash,
  The uniforms and things :
The sunlit sabre's glittering flash

(When all unused to human hash !)
  To me a pleasure brings.

So much I love the pomp and show
  That warlike men display,
I once had half a mind to go
Where swords must strike and blood must flow,
  And some must run away.

But well I knew their lot is hard
  Who through the South do roam ;
And rather than be maimed or scarred
I 've joined the glorious, gallant Guard,
  Who vow to stay at Home.

So down Broadway I proudly ride,
  Through heat and dust and noise ;
My dress-sword jingles at my side,
And I am puffed by martial pride,
  And chaffed by vulgar boys.

Let others fight, let others fall,
  Let others wear the bays ;

But at the military ball
Let me adorn the festive hall,
   Where gimp and buttons blaze.

Then fill your glasses full and free,
   And drink the health that's right,—
To him that joins my company
And only wants, like me, to be
   A Broadway carpet-knight.

'T is ours to keep well-fed and warm;
   We scorn all poor supplies;
We fear no bloody battle's storm,
We wear a nice new uniform
   And tend our shops likewise.

So now, brave boys, I move that when
   The war has drained our land
Of good and valiant fighting men,
Should we be called, I move that then
   We instantly disband.

A VOICE FROM ON DECK.

GOOD Mister Welles, my mind is set,
  And I must say my say or die:
I never minded getting wet;
  Why should you keep me dry?

On sprees I never used to go;
  I took my ration — *quantum suff* —
But then I am a Salt, you know,
  And salt is thirsty stuff.

When nausea would not let me sup, —
  When winds did blow and skies did frown, —
Grog often kept my spirits up,
  And kept my victuals down.

Each Salt that roves the briny wave
  Will tell you I have truly sung;

And what you at the spigot save
  Will leak out at the bung.

Since you 've pronounced the fatal word,
  Our fun goes never quite so far:
And pray, what could be more absurd —
  A sober jolly Tar?

I used to sing a merry stave,
  However loud the tempest roared;
But now my energies I save, —
  There 's not a stave on board.

Without my grog I feel afraid
  To venture where I 've little room;
Yet 't is a portion of my trade
  To go upon a boom.

Now, Mister Welles, I 'll say good by,
  With hopes that, in a little while,
We water-dogs may not be dry, —
  We jolly Tars may smile!

THE PLAINT OF THE POSTAGE-STAMP.

I'M a very dirty little Stamp;
    My back is gummed, my face is dimly blurred;
And yet I am, in commerce, cot, and camp,
    Familiar as the well-known household word.
Yet O, to think that I should ever be
Converted into legal currency!

Now on an envelope I'm not so bad,
    And I take letters through both cheap and
        neat;
Sticking to one thing was a way I had,
    But now I stick to everything I meet:
And O, to think that I could ever be
Passed in the place of metal currency!

To do my duty I did ne'er refuse;
    But woe is me! for I have fallen low;

I'm passed for vulgar drinks and oyster-stews,
  And dirty shaves,—'t is that that sticks me so!
Alas! alas! that I should ever be
A victim to the dearth of currency!

Thumbing and gumming have quite worn me out;
  I'm drab and dingy now, instead of red;
My back is weak, and soon, without a doubt,
  If I am passed much more I'll lose my head.
O sorry day! when I did chance to be
Put to the use of baser currency!

1862.

THE WAR-POET'S LAMENT.

WHEN lovers and sweethearts and house-
  holds were sundered,
  And lurid clouds darkened the bright south-
    ern sky,
When cannon and mortar and musketry thun-
    dered,
And tyrants in foreign lands trembled and won-
    dered,
  How happy and busy a poet was I!

I sought no laborious plots and devices;
  Battle-rhymes almost unconsciously come;
You can chop 'em off neatly, to order, in
    slices,
Charging — and getting — most fabulous prices,
  If lavish of "death-dealing cannon" and "drum."

O, how I revelled in visions of battle:—
  "Blood," and "destruction," and "victory's
    shout,"
"Piled heaps of slain," and the "horrid death-
    rattle"!...
Now I must poetize small-talk and tattle;
  Peace has come in, and my trade has gone
    out!

What shall I sing, whose sole stock has been
    Glory?
  How shall I turn from the worship of Mars?
How leave a field so productive and gory?
Changing to tranquil and pastoral story?
  How shall I pay for my wine and cigars?

Such a *dénouement* I hardly expected,
  Till the sad morn when I rose from my bed,
Saw the white temple that Peace had erected,
Found my last war-song politely rejected,
  Myself in despair, and with never a red!

Ah, it is mournful! our soldiers and sailors
   Furnish no longer a theme for my pen:
What foes we have left we confide to our jailers,
And — gad! I 'll write rhymes for the popular
    tailors,
   And sing of brave garments instead of brave
    men!

SHODDY.

TERRIBLE times of sorrow and need;
Times to make hearts of adamant bleed;
Times that seem to have been decreed
To chasten our wayward nation:
Fathers and brothers thinning away,
Bread growing scarcer every day,
Famine to pinch and sword to slay—
'T is a woful situation!

But, even as Nero, in days of old,
Unmoved, heard Roman fire-bells tolled,
And saw the machines that rattled and rolled
To the scene of the great disaster,
The while he rosined his fiddle-bow,
And played some classic " Rob Ridley, O!"
So we make merry, while all things go
To the dickens, faster, and faster!

Parties, sociables, visits and calls,
Operas, hops, and Russian balls,
'Mid broken pillars and tottering walls,
    Enough to bewilder a body ;
Silver and gold, and gems of the mine,
Satin to rustle and silk to shine,
Feathers and fuss and frippery fine —
    The paraphernalia of Shoddy.

Carriages flash through the crowded street,
Flunkeys in livery stiff on each seat,
Buttoned and caped from head to feet —
    Most solemn, majestical flunkeys ;
And "tigers," to let down the steps with a bow —
Learned, only tigers and Heaven know how !
Dressed up in a fashion I must allow
    Like that of the organ monkeys.

The ladies, who walk when the weather is fair,
Show marvellous tastes, with a marvellous air.
Nothing can be too splendid to wear ;
    Too gaudy, too fine, or too funny ;

For credit is good, if prices are high,
And a government nod, or wink of the eye,
Can pile up "greenbacks" clear to the sky,—
  "Greenbacks" being Shoddy for money.

So yellows, and blues, and scarlets, gay
Go sweeping the pavements every day,
Making a rainbow of poor Broadway,
    With a glare that is really stunning;
And even the churches where fashion goes
Are a mass of follies and furbelows,
Flirtation and foolery under the rose,
    Past even the serpent's cunning.

While Shoddy over its turtle gloats,
Our soldiers shiver in rotten coats,
And our tars go down in their leaky boats,
    The victims of contract building;
And poverty starves in its wretched slums,
Or freezes to death when the north wind comes,
While Shoddy is picking the sweetest plums
    From its bed of gingerbread gilding.

But what cares Shoddy for all these things?
Shoddy, the richest of paper kings:
Shoddy, who dances, fiddles, and sings
    On the crater of wild inflation?
What does he care? Not a sou-markee!
He fattens and battens in luxury,
As if his reign were a thing to be
    Of eternal perpetuation.

But Damocles' sword hangs overhead:
Justice may sleep, but she is not dead;
"Vengeance is mine!" the Lord hath said;
    And soon, at the end of the story,
Fruitiest wine shall be bitterest gall;
Silk and satin make shroud and pall;
Truth shall rise and Shoddy shall fall,—
    To the nation's lasting glory!

1864.